Two more damaged ships followed, each listing, the fifth badly down by the bows, the sixth, half a mile astern and trying to keep up. Two huge gashes showed in her side, the edges of her wounds also blackened by the heat from the explosions: she was the other surviving container ship whose poop deck had been converted into a pad for her Sea Harriers – Trevellion could see the remains of one which must have received the blast from the missile explosion. . . .

Also by John Wingate in Sphere Books:

FRIGATE
SUBMARINE

Carrier

JOHN WINGATE

SPHERE BOOKS LIMITED
30–32 Gray's Inn Road, London WC1X 8JL

First published in Great Britain by
Weidenfeld & Nicolson 1981
Copyright © John Wingate 1981
Published by Sphere Books Ltd 1982

TRADE
MARK

Set in Baskerville

Reproduced, printed and bound in Great Britain by
Hazell Watson & Viney Ltd, Aylesbury, Bucks

Acknowledgements

Carrier, the second book in the trilogy, has been made possible through the co-operation and kindness of many friends.

I wish particularly to thank the Naval Staff in the Ministry of Defence and all those in the Service, at sea, in the air and ashore, serving and retired, who made my task so agreeable.

To my counsellors and friends who, as in *Frigate*, so freely gave their time, encouragement and advice to check the manuscript, I wish to express my sincere gratitude.

Finally, I am extremely grateful for the continued encouragement and counsel given by Admiral of the Fleet Sir Edward Ashmore, GCB, DSC, during all stages in the writing of this book.

JOHN WINGATE

'*After all, it is the men who win the battles...*'

Admiral of the Fleet Viscount
Cunningham of Hyndhope

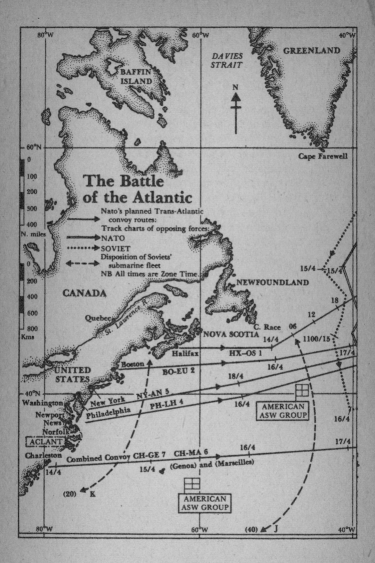

The Battle of the Atlantic

Nato's planned Trans-Atlantic convoy routes:
Track charts of opposing forces:
→ NATO
•••••→ SOVIET
Disposition of Soviets' submarine fleet
NB All times are Zone Time.

N. miles
0
100
200
300
400

0
200
400
600
800
Kms

80°W   60°W   40°W

GREENLAND

DAVIES STRAIT

N

BAFFIN ISLAND

60°N

Cape Farewell

NEWFOUNDLAND

CANADA

Quebec

St. Lawrence

NOVA SCOTIA

C. Race   06   12   18

15/4   15/4

1100/15   17/4

HX–OS 1   14/4   16/4

Halifax

Boston   BO-EU 2   18/4

UNITED STATES

NY-AN 5   16/4   AMERICAN ASW GROUP   16/4

Washington   New York   PH-LH 4
Newport   Philadelphia   16/4   17/4
Norfolk

ACLANT   Combined Convoy CH-GE 7   CH-MA 6   16/4   17/4

Charleston   14/4   15/4   (Genoa) and (Marseilles)

(20)   K   AMERICAN ASW GROUP

(40) ◄ J

40°N

80°W   60°W   40°W

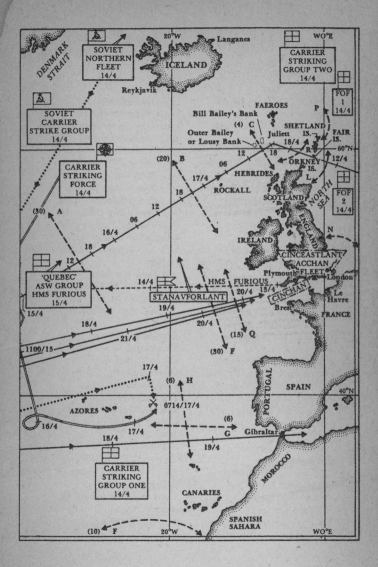

Glossary

ACLANT *Allied Command Atlantic*
AEW *Airborne Early Warning*
AIRCENT *Allied Air Forces Central Europe*
ALC *Armed Landing Craft*
Anvil *Soviet Sub-surface Air Missile*
ASI *Air Speed Indicator*
ASW *Anti-Submarine Warfare*
AWC *Air Warfare Co-ordination*
AWO *Advanced War Officer*
CAH *Carrier Aircraft, Helicopter*
CAP *Combat Air Patrol*
CINCEASTLANT *C-in-C East Atlantic*
CINCCHAN *C-in-C Channel and North Sea*
COMBALTAP *Commander Allied Forces Baltic Approaches*
COMSTANAVFORLANT *Commander Standing Naval Force Atlantic*
COMSTRIGRUTWO *Commander Striking Group Two*
COMSUBEASTLANT *Commander Submarine Forces Eastern Atlantic*
DDG *Destroyer, Guided Missile*
DLG *Frigate, Guided Missile*
ECM *Electronic Countermeasure*
ECCM *Electronic Counter-Countermeasure*
ELINT *Electronic Intelligence*
EW *Electronic Warfare*
FCS *Flight Control System*
FCSS *Fast Combat Support Ship*
GDB *Gun Director, Blind*
HCO *Helicopter Controller*
HE *High Explosive*, also *Hydrophone Effect*

ICBM *Intercontinental Ballistic Missile*
IFF *Identification Friend or Foe*
LRMP *Long Range Maritime Patrol*
MAC *Merchant Aircraft Carrier*
MEM *Marine Engineer Mechanic*
MEO *Marine Engineer Officer*
MLA *Mean Line of Advance*
NDB *Nuclear Depth Bomb*
PMO *Principal Medical Officer*
PPI *Plan Position Indicator*
PWO *Principal Warfare Officer*
RAS *Replenishment at Sea*
SACLANT *Supreme Allied Commander Atlantic*
SAR *Search and Rescue*
SATCOM *Satellite Communications*
SLBM *Submarine-Launched Ballistic Missile (USA); Sea-Launched Ballistic Missile (Nato)*
SOBS *Senior Observer*
Sosus *Sound Surveillance System*
SPLOT *Senior Pilot*
SSBN *Submarine, Strategic Ballistic Missile Nuclear*
SSK *Submarine, Diesel*
STANAVFORCHAN *Standing Naval Force Channel*
Stass *Ships' Towed Array Surveillance System*
Ts and Ps *Temperatures and Pressures*
UKADGE *United Kingdom Air Defence Ground Environment*
VCNS *Vice-Chief Naval Staff*
VLCC *Very Large Crude Carrier*
V/STOL *Vertical or Short Take-Off and Landing*

1

Cornwall, 12 April: It was the nausea that came with the dawn which woke Allie Gamble to semi-consciousness. She tried to sleep, curling herself against Hob, feeling the stubble of his chin against her shoulder – but it was no good: she had not felt so sick for as long as she could remember.

She slithered from between the sheets and tiptoed to the dormer window tucked into the gables of Leat Cottage, their first real home, and smiled to herself as she edged back the primrose curtains: there was the usual old blackbird, whistling his morning hymn. She turned towards the bed, her eyes lingering on Hob's profile: he was like a child lying there, relaxed in sleep...

Hob had told her only the bare outlines of what happened during that terrible Wednesday of 2 January. She could never forget that day and night waiting for the telephone call from MOD: watching him asleep like this, it was impossible to brush away the fleeting image of death, of Rollo Dalglish and Hob in the blazing Lynx – and it was to Rollo, Hob's captain and observer, that Hob owed his life. Rollo was dead when the American frigate had picked him up, lashed to Hob's life raft.

Allie jumped as the alarm clock shrilled by her side of the bed.

Hob was awake immediately, his arms outstretched to her. His bushy black eyebrows beneath the fair hair which stood up like a shaving brush lent his face a humorous, quizzical look which belied his toughness. Though Hob was gentle to her, he was ambitious – the most professional person she had ever met. He frightened her sometimes: flying came first in his life, even before herself. She stepped back as he tried to encircle her thighs with his hands.

'Lieutenant Gamble!' she scowled down at him where he lay, bare-chested, blue-chinned, eyes laughing, those blue-green eyes which missed nothing. 'You're duty pilot today. You need every bit of strength and concentration.'

She watched the wide smile slowly spreading across his face, leaned down to kiss him on the cheek as he crooked his arms behind his tousled head. 'You've forgotten what's happening today.'

'No, I haven't. First Sea Lord's visit.' Hob turned towards the window. 'What's the day like?'

'Jolly grockling weather,' she smiled.

It was only six days since Easter and already the grockles – or tourists – had provided round-the-clock work for the Search and Rescue Squadron, the Wessex boys. She was thankful that Hob had gone back to Sea Kings after *Icarus* and that he was again with his friends in 814 Squadron: he needed people round him after that awful night. He had loathed the publicity which descended on him after his DSC, when Captain Trevellion and the other survivors were honoured at the Palace. Though the tragedy was over three months ago, it was still vivid in both their minds.

'Anyway, Allie, the Sea Kings are lucky, combining two jobs in one. At least, I'm not forced to wait in the base like the SAR crew.'

It did not feel like wartime. It was only as Hob glanced at the two stripes on his sleeve that he remembered that it wasn't peacetime either – a pregnant limbo had settled over the whole world since 2 January. He braced his shoulders. He'd had enough of introspection and could leave the future to those who were unlucky enough to have its destiny in their hands. The abortive summit meeting two days ago at Geneva had been bad news. Meanwhile, he had his work which, thank goodness, was never the same two days running at Culdrose – and he eased the car into the ditch to allow an empty school bus to squeeze by him in the lane leading into Wendron.

The morning was brisk, the fluffy clouds streaming in ragged battalions from the Atlantic. There had been another late frost and the hedgerows were grey and silver where they lined the fields. The sweet scent from the gorse spikes nodding in the gateways wafted through his open window: a good flying day, if the fog kept away.

814's duty pilot was required an hour earlier than usual; the grockles were giving trouble already. The First Sea Lord's visit would be affected if Hob did not get a move on – but he was chuffed he had picked the job: a good augury for Lieutenant Gamble's future, as well as confirmation that he had satisfied the instructor during his Sea King conversion course. Duggie Mann, the Squadron CO, had hinted that he might be asking for Hob as his senior pilot in *Furious*. Hob should know any day now, because 814 Squadron was joining the carrier on Monday when she came into Mount's Bay.

Culdrose was still miles ahead but his bleeper was sounding in his pocket. He put his foot down: he would be late for the briefing if he didn't shift a bit. . . . He couldn't help thinking about Allie, three months pregnant now; that made the birth due this October, didn't it? And he grinned stupidly as he turned down to the town and Penzance.

Allie's face, beloved above all others – nothing particularly beautiful in a conventional way, but unique with her elf-like, elusive charm: the tiny pointed chin and the hazel eyes in her pale, serene face contrasted with her black hair and clearly reflected her character.

Hob Gamble still had a grin on his face as he slammed his car door and hurried into 814's block. The briefing had already begun and the senior pilot's scowl was not the most welcoming. The rest of the crew were already in their flying gear.

'I'll repeat the weather for you, Lieutenant Gamble,' the senior pilot said. Hob jotted down the details: deteriorating, but vis. ought to be holding for an hour or two, if fog did not clamp down when the warm air stream crossed the Atlantic coast. 'We've had to bring your Sea King forward as the stand-by SAR, Hob, because things are getting out of hand a bit.'

Gamble nodded: they'd rather have something to do than wait for the First Sea Lord's inspection which was disrupting flying training this forenoon. The duty Wessex was already out on search-and-rescue and Wessex 779 was standing by to pick up the First Sea Lord from Redruth.

'That's all,' the senior pilot concluded. 'You can start your pre-flight checks and drills as soon as you've manned your aircraft.'

Hob hurried down to the changing-room, where he put on his

flying and survival gear, his crew lounging around him, their bone domes in their hands. Hob listened in silence to his crew: the second pilot, a young sub training for front-line; the observer, a trained SAR diver but still not front-line; and Hermann, the ginger-haired, burly West German aircrewman on loan through Nato.

Hob moved out on to the tarmac. They followed him, strapping their helmets as they approached the huge helicopter, ten tons of complicated machinery and electronics with its twin Rolls-Royce Gnome engines. Hob gave his customary visual check: the naval blue paint of the cab gleamed in the fitful April sunlight, the number 827 and the snarling tiger's head of 814 Squadron showed starkly on the side of the fuselage. The yellow tenders stood clear to the side where the engineers were waiting – with over three hundred technicians to keep these helos in the air, Hob never felt uneasy about the quality of maintenance – a factor which *did* concern the flyers. There was a rocklike thoroughness about the air engineering department.

They climbed on board, strapped in and went through their pre-take-off checks. Hob allowed the sub to do the work.

'All ready in the back?' Hob was asking the observer and aircrewman, when the sub chipped in:

'The whanger's going, Hob. Scramble!'

The duty coastguard officer in the crewroom had received a report from Black Head that a child with a dog in an inflatable canoe were in difficulties off Hyrlas Rock.

The brief details came in as Hob lifted 827 swiftly, swooping left across the airfield. As he climbed to two hundred feet, the emerald green of the turf dividing the concrete runways of the airfield began to merge with the haphazard fields of Cornwall. A map reference of the incident was passed to the observer, and then Hob was heading for Goonhilly which was already showing up to the south-east. Normally, the Kilcobben Cove lifeboat under the Lizard would have been called, but the Black Head coastguard had already alerted Culdrose that minutes would count. The child was being blown into the confused water off the point, where the tidal stream was running hard.

'There it is!'

The sub had spotted the craft, a blue and red object bobbing in the breaking seas between Hyrlas Rock and the cliffs of the black islet encircled by the swirling, frothing seas. Hob began to take 827 down into the hover.

'All ready in the back.' Hermann croaked through the intercom: 'Opening the door.'

The drill continued, the results of months of training in automatic response to emergency, each man concentrating on his own task. Hob was watching the cliff, one eye on his lateral drift, the other on his heading.

'Twenty feet,' the sub called.

The observer had left his seat to man the winch. Hermann was already in the sling and was sitting on the lip of the door.

'Right two ... back one ... steady ...'

The crisp directions from the observer conned Hob directly above the casualty, while Hermann was lowered on the wire. Hob kept his eyes fixed on his marks ahead, his fingers caressing the collective. The sub in the second pilot's seat was doing well, calmly monitoring the readings.

'Up three ... that's good ... steady ... steady.'

Hob could only guess at what was going on twenty feet below in those galloping waves; with each minute, 827 was drifting down upon the outlying islet. Hob would have to lift her soon or the blades would be at risk. These two-hundred-foot winch wires were good news, providing he could plumb the casualty.

'Hooked on.' The observer could not conceal the tension in his voice. 'Hoisting.'

It seemed ages before they rumpled the pathetic little figure over the lip of the door. From the terse snippets through the intercom, Hob heard that the observer was giving the girl expelled air resuscitation.

'She's alive, but only just,' the observer reported a few minutes later. 'Her puppy's still in the canoe.'

Hob was tense, watching the jagged needles of the rock-face creeping nearer. A cloud of gulls shivered against the ironstone, their squawking protestations inaudible from where Hob sat immobile inside his perspex cockpit. All depended upon the speed of the winchman, and the relative value of a puppy's life against £2½ millions' worth of chopper and five lives.

'Go to the back,' Hob said to the second pilot. 'I've got her.' Out of the corner of his eye he glimpsed the sub unsnapping his harness, then picking his way though the maze of sensitive controls as if he was tiptoeing across red-hot needles. Half a minute later, the observer was crouching over his unconscious patient, while the sub lowered Hermann; less than a minute, and the puppy was recovered. The blade tips seemed to be scraping the tufts of sea pinks which sprinkled the gull colony. The observer shouted, hurting Hob's ears:

'That's it, Hob. Both inboard. Shutting the door.'

Hob Gamble eased the cab to seaward, saw the darker blue of the deeper water gliding beneath his feet. He gently pulled her up to fifty feet, then waited for them in the back to sort themselves out and the second pilot to regain his seat. As soon as the observer had given a heading Sea King 827 was on her way, forging ahead at 120 knots across the rolling countryside towards Truro.

Apart from the stereotyped drill for conversation, Hob silently coaxed the Sea King to her limits, the machine canted forwards to thrust up Carrick Roads towards the narrowing banks of the River Fal. Then came the rounded, dark woods lapping the muddy banks; the creeks and the fields – and, at last, the buildings of Treliske hospital appeared suddenly in front of him.

He touched down 827 with more of a jolt than usual. The waiting stretchermen took the child away quickly, clamping an oxygen mask over the tiny, blue face.

'Back to base, Hob,' the observer reported. 'We're wanted on the VIP spot by 1125: you'd better get a shift on.'

Hob applied the lift and took her up.

'What's up?' he asked.

'They won't tell me,' the observer said. 'I suspect it's a ferry job.'

Hob glanced at the clock on the instrument panel: 1107. The VIP spot was ominous. . . .

'Hey, you guys,' he passed through the common line. 'You'd better spruce the old cab up. I reckon we're booked for the First Sea Lord.'

He did not catch what Hermann said to the observer but

there was laughter and a great deal of scrabbling going on in the back end.

As they flew to Culdrose each man was silent with his own thoughts, hoping that on arrival at the airfield the news from Treliske might compensate for their efforts. Now Hob could see the grey hangars, the plush buildings of the residential complex. He turned across the tower and took her down towards the VIP spot where a huddle of senior officers was peering upwards.

2

London, 12 April. Even the platforms of Paddington station had a touch of spring about them this morning where the light of dawn was filtering through the grimy roof. There was zest, too, in the step of the distinguished-looking officer in the bridge coat who strode through the barrier. The ticket collector, impressed by the admiral's uniform, touched the peak of his cap. He did not often check the ticket of a full admiral, even in these crazy days.

Admiral Sir Anthony Layde, GCB, MVO, carried nothing with him. For him, today was a day for re-charging his cerebral batteries, as well as for encouraging his airmen.

'Morning, Alan.'

His naval assistant, a captain, held open the door of the first-class carriage.

'Makes a change to flying, sir.' He led the way to the compartment and slid back the door. 'Gives you a bit of slack.'

The First Sea Lord settled himself into the corner seat, idly watched the platform slipping by, and noted the guard yawning as he waved the driver off.

'You should get some zeds in,' Layde muttered. 'It'll be a long day.' He smiled briefly at his naval assistant, who had been working all hours during these hectic weeks. 'I want a few hours' peace for some solid thinking – that's why I'm going down to Culdrose by train.'

'A Jetstream's lined up to take you back, sir. The captain says his pilots want to fly you back. It's a good training aeroplane.'

Layde nodded. The Penzance express soon began to pick up speed, rattling through the suburbs and gliding out into the green of the spring countryside around Windsor, where the banks of the Thames were lined with pollarded willows. Dawn in the English countryside still did something to him – and he

16

leaned forwards to follow a brace of snipe, dipping and tripping across the marshes. Alan was already asleep...

The First Sea Lord slipped his diary from his reefer pocket: he needed time to think. He had grown into the habit of acting as the bluff sea dog: he enjoyed playing the part, but it was a pardonable fault in his position as chief of the Royal Navy. Today's fleet was impersonal enough, with its fetish for replacing leadership by 'management' – a fundamental error which he was trying to remedy.

Everything had depended on the summit meeting at Geneva two days ago. He would have been a fool to have expected any other conclusion. He had nearly reached his retirement but the *Icarus* incident, as the media now termed the affair, had ended any chance of enjoying the serenity of his Herefordshire home. He flicked the pages of his diary backwards...

From time to time Layde moved restlessly – what a woeful indictment of man's condition were the repeated acts of aggression and counter-aggression catalogued in the last three months of his diary. He felt the train slowing as the first of Reading's suburbs flashed past the window. The sun was low above the horizon: the wet gutters were glistening pink.

Two days ago, the world summit meeting at Geneva had dissolved in confusion – the crisis everyone was dreading. The Americans were at Red Alert, their Sixth Fleet was concentrating south-west of Cyprus. The Governor of Gib must be having sleepless nights.

Yesterday, Friday 11 April, the Americans and Nato had told the Soviets that Europe would be reinforced forthwith along every trade route leading to that continent. Last night, Moscow retorted bluntly that if the convoys sailed, they would be attacked. The sailing of the convoys would be considered by the Soviets as an act of aggression against the Warsaw Pact, which had no intention of attacking across the central plains of Europe – providing Nato's divisions remained static. The convoys, unmolested but heavily guarded, still lay at anchor from Halifax to Charleston.

As the train slid to a halt at Reading, Layde caught sight of a group of senior railway officials peering at the windows speeding past them. He watched one of them hurrying to the door of the first-class carriage. Layde glanced across at his exhausted assistant:

'Better see what they want, Alan.'

The naval assistant hurried along the corridor, then returned to poke his head round the door.

'It's VCNS, sir,' he reported. 'He's on the phone.'

Layde asked to be left alone in the stationmaster's office.

'Yes, Charles.'

'I thought you'd better know at once, sir, in case you want to return immediately. Director-General of Intelligence has just been through. . . .' Charles seemed worried by the open line. He was barely audible.

'What's up?'

'At 0515 this morning an unidentified number of Bulgarian divisions crossed the Turkish and Greek frontiers. They're heading for the Straits and Salonika.'

Layde stood silently for a full five seconds. Then he said:

'That makes up our minds for us, Charles.'

'Shall I send a car for you, sir?'

'Why?'

'I thought –'

'My airmen are the one hope we've got at this moment. I'll want a sitrep when I reach Culdrose.'

'Aye, aye, sir.'

The First Sea Lord put down the receiver slowly. He stood for a moment, his hands stuffed into his reefer pockets, then strode purposefully back to his carriage.

Salisbury, Exeter, Plymouth – the journey seemed endless. To smother his impatience Layde sharpened his thinking on his naval assistant. Alan was a good companion and no yes-man. Looking back on it all, they agreed that the dangerous days had begun when the West, divided and confused by the Afghanistan *fait accompli*, had not understood that unity came before self-interest, and the crisis had accelerated from that point. The Soviet leaders had made it abundantly clear that they aimed to destroy the West; they often said so publicly. They could do so by two methods: through subversion in every facet of Western national life – economic, social and defence – and, if that failed, by using force to cut Atlantic sea-lanes. During the stalemate

18

since January, they had tacitly accepted that a decision restricted to war at sea was preferable to any other battleground. They had posed their argument with brutal candour.

Assuming that the superpowers were compelled to fight, even at the expense of destroying civilization on this planet, the outcome of a land battle on the central plains of Europe would depend on whether the armies of the West could be reinforced from the American arsenal on the other side of the Atlantic.

If the Soviets were to win the Atlantic, by denying the sea-lanes to Nato reinforcements, it would be pointless for Nato to resist on the central plains. But if Nato won the Atlantic, it would be illogical for Russia to invade Europe because she would, in the end, be overwhelmed as the American reinforcements began rolling into the European ports.

The corollary was as brutal: whichever side won this battle of the Atlantic, Europe could be spared the holocaust of land warfare, a condition which the superpowers preferred: a devastated continent was a liability to both contestants, whoever nominally won. Thus went the Soviet argument, but the unknown factor was the quality of Soviet naval technology: how good were their ships, their men?

The side who knew most about the other's EW would win the short, savage contest – and the Soviets had not been parsimonious with their espionage investment. Communications and surveillance were the key, which was why Nato had been shadowing the Soviet ships and submarines for so many years – and vice versa.

The Russians depended on two types of satellites for watching the West: those which provided the data for Soviet electronic intelligence, and their radar satellites for surprise detection. Electronic warfare – each side jamming and confusing the other – would be the decisive weapon, although there were many imponderables. Only hot war could divulge the extent of their armoury. Had the Russians broken through the ASW barrier? They were known to be working on an entirely different system to sonar – perhaps by sensing the trace elements in coolant discharges from nuclear submarines. Had their submarines, armed with the mysterious Anvil, mastered our main counter, the ASW helicopter? Would they use their appalling superiority in biological and chemical warfare?

'Truro, Truro, next stop Redruth, Penzance,' the station loudspeakers blared. The naval assistant began collecting his papers.

The size of the Soviet submarine effort still kept Layde awake at nights – over four hundred known to be at sea, 250 of them nukes, with wartime construction running at thirty annually. British intelligence insisted that there existed over 250 fleet attack submarines whose role was ASW; their first job was to trail the fifty American and four British SSBNs from the moment they left port – and to destroy them, if war came. Their second priority was to destroy Nato warships, the prime targets being the strike carriers whose aircraft could at any moment reach deep into the Soviet Union. Their third priority was to sink our trans-Atlantic shipping. SALT had limited the Soviets to sixty-two Deltas and Yankees but the principal effect of this was a massive Soviet building programme for fleet attack submarines with which to counter Nato's strategic missile boats. The world could see, at last, the reason for the Soviet's gigantic submarine effort.

In the seventies, the Soviet's long-range boats, the Yankees and Deltas, with their improved missiles, could reach the United States from within Russian waters in the Barents, while the Golfs and Hotels covered China and Europe; their Echos could deal with Nato support ships and amphibious targets. Then the Americans went one better by producing their huge Ohios armed with sub-surface Trident missiles. But the race had only begun....

The world's first underwater battleship, of the Russian Typhoon class, was at sea in the early eighties. Displacing twenty thousand tons dived, they were larger than the first of our CAHs, *Invincible* and *Illustrious*, the first purpose-built Sea Harrier ASW carriers. Fired from the safety of the Barents Sea the Typhoons' SS-N-18 missiles could reach Charleston, Washington, Chicago and all Canada. From the Sea of Japan, Sydney was pin-pointed; from the Sea of Okhotsk (the Kuriles), the whole of the American and Canadian Pacific seaboard was menaced. The Typhoons could with impunity lay waste any city in the world; while on the loose in the oceans they could be supplied by any of the Soviet 'protectorate' bases from Conakry to Mozambique, from Djibouti to Cienfuegos.

Layde's naval assistant was on his feet and holding the door open.

'Redruth, sir,' he announced.

3

Culdrose, 12 April. 'Glad you could make it, sir.'

'Not even this morning's news would have kept me away, Derek. I want to see for myself whether you're ready.'

'Well, sir, it's 1939 all over again. We've been doing what we can but it's too little too late.'

Captain Derek Quincey, commanding officer of HMS *Seahawk*, the Royal Naval Air Station at Culdrose, was the fine young officer Layde remembered as senior observer in the old carrier the First Sea Lord had commanded some years ago. On the way across the tarmac to the officers lined up to meet the First Sea Lord, Quincey handed Layde a signal.

'I hope you can stick to the programme in spite of this, sir,' he said.

Layde glanced at it, then reread it with care.

'This is it, Derek,' he said. 'We've work to do.'

Layde felt relieved now they knew where they stood. The first convoys had sailed and the Soviets had been as good as their word. Three ships had been sunk by submarine attack and the convoy escorts were retaliating. There were confirmed reports of a Soviet nuclear-powered submarine in the Western Channel. The minesweeper who had picked her up had lost contact and Sea Kings from HMS *Furious*, now closing Land's End, were taking up the search. . . .

'Stick to the programme,' Layde said, 'but reverse the procedure a bit. I'll start with the Squadrons, but don't interfere with SAR and flying training.'

Culdrose was the largest helicopter base in Europe and the biggest Royal Naval Air Station. The Admiralty had shown foresight in 1944 when it had bought the land upon which the modern hangars were built, the new buildings blending into the Cornish landscape now the camouflage was weathering. Layde started his tour with the SAR Wessexes, then was driven on to

the front-line and training squadrons. The base was humming.
VCNS had wasted no time: 814 Squadron was flying-on before
dawn on Sunday, a day earlier than planned, when *Furious*
would dash into Mount's Bay.

They showed Layde the back-up services, the vital support
which kept these highly complicated machines safely in the
air: these technicians were as proud of themselves as the fine
bunch of aircrewmen, observers and pilots to whom he had
already talked. There was a grim purpose about Culdrose now,
and this determination showed in many of the young men's
faces.

Layde paid lightning visits to the various schools, and
inspected the heart of the place, the air engineering department; the specialists – the air traffic control and the simulator
teams; the unique bird control unit which used falcons to keep
the runways clear of gulls and other birds; the met. office in the
Naval Air Command's weather centre; and the medical and
dental teams which were so essential to these finely-tuned men
who stayed alive solely through the speed of their reflexes. He
wished that he could have spared more time with the Wrens
and the supply and secretarial personnel who cemented the
whole outfit together. There were also civilians, without whom
the base could not operate – specialists who kept the simulator
functioning day in, day out; the Helston men and the contrac-
tors....

'Time for coffee, sir, before you go? The Jetstream is
standing-by,' Quincey said as Layde's car drew up to the
wardroom at one end of the modern *Seahawk* centre, the huge
accommodation complex which housed, fed and looked after
the 2,600 officers, ratings and Wrens.

To Layde's right was the admin. block, the nearest door of
which led to the captain's offices. A tall lieutenant-commander
was taking the two steps at time. He halted in front of Captain
Quincey and saluted:

'MOD on the scrambler, sir. VCNS wishes to speak personally
to the First Sea Lord.'

Sir Anthony nodded and beckoned the captain to accompany
him. He shook his head as Quincey pushed a chair towards
him. 'Bad news, Charles?'

'Bloody, sir. I still can't credit it.' The line was clear, but VCNS paused uncertainly.

'Get on with it.'

'In the early hours,' VCNS said tensely, 'it must have been about the same time as the Bulgarians' attack, the Devonport security police were fooled by several impersonators. Without going into details, sir, the police who patrol the nuclear submarine refuelling and refitting complex were attacked and overpowered just before the day shift came on.'

'What's happened?' Layde demanded impatiently.

'D'you remember, sir, during your Devonport inspection, you looked at the two new submarine dry docks?'

'Yes . . .'

'Saboteurs – there must have been divers among 'em – have shattered the hinges on both dock gates.' The voice at the other end paused, tense.

'Are the gates inoperative?' Layde asked, thinking of the huge steel flaps imprisoning Britain's newest nuclear submarines.

'Totally, sir. I don't know for how long, but they could be jammed for days. They've also put the operating winches out of action.'

'So *Saracen* is boxed in?' The First Sea Lord paused, then added: 'Her dock's not flooded?'

'No, sir. The gate held, but they killed her sentries. Thank God, sir you insisted on getting *Sealion* to sea, in spite of her defects.'

Layde was stunned by the catastrophe: a handful of determined saboteurs had put out of action half of Britain's nuclear submarine force, even before the war had officially started. The Soviets were playing no longer. 'Faslane all right?'

'Nothing so far, sir. Better security.'

There was a long silence and then VCNS came back:

'You there, sir?'

'Come to Rule of Engagement Two, Charles.' Layde paused, then ordered: 'Put the Navy and the yards on Alert One, war footing, whatever the politicians are doing.'

'The PM's speaking at noon, sir.'

'Good. I'm returning at once, but I'll call at Devonport on my way up.' He raised his eyebrows as he glanced at Quincey. 'Thanks, Charles. Keep holding the fort.' He slapped down the receiver.

'I'll take you to Guz by Sea King, sir.'

'Thanks,' Layde said. 'Can your Jetstream take me on from Devonport?'

'Yes, sir. I'll have it standing by. The helicopter can take you straight into the dockyard.'

The captain led the way to the wardroom. As he stood by the door, Layde said:

'Before I go, I'd like to speak to your ship's company on your broadcast system, Derek. They ought to be the first to know we're virtually at war: they're right up-front.'

'Spot 7,' the visual control ordered. 'Your passengers are standing-by.'

Hob took Sea King 827 straight in, across the eastern boundary of Helston. No one spoke. There must be more on their slop chit, because Flight Planning had already passed their routeing instructions to Devonport.

'Ts and Ps good,' the second pilot reported, as he completed the landing checks. 'Brake off.'

'Harnesses all round?' Hob asked.

'Checked. Ready in the back,' the observer called. Hob dropped the duty Sea King towards spot 7. Out of the corner of his eye he could see four figures standing at one side on the tarmac, two of whom were in flying gear. 827 hovered for a couple of seconds then flounced down on to the spot.

'I'll welcome the Old Man,' Hob said, handing over the helicopter to the second pilot.

Hermann slid back the side door. As Hob gingerly eased himself between the pilots' seats, he glimpsed the two passengers climbing into the back of the aircraft. The younger of the two senior officers stayed with the aircrewman, while the elder (presumably the First Sea Lord, by the size of him) was being eased for'd into the passenger's seat. The intercom lines were plugged in and, stooping like a couple of hunchbacks, the two

25

men faced each other, their eyes meeting beneath their grotesque helmets.

'Lieutenant Gamble?' the admiral asked.

Hob tried to slice him off a smart salute. 'Yes, sir. I'm afraid we've kept you waiting.'

'Thank you, Gamble. I didn't think I'd have the chance of congratulating you myself on your gong. Seems some time ago, I expect.'

'Yes, sir. Another world.'

'Thanks ... that's fine. I won't bother you any more.'

Hob climbed back into his pilot's seat.

'I have control...'

'You have control,' the second pilot acknowledged and then they were again soaring over Helston. As soon as he had cleared the airfield, Hob turned towards St Anthony Head. The observer passed the heading and they settled down for the flight.

'Quite happy, sir?' Hob asked. 'ETA Devonport 1205.'

The deep voice replied with a touch of gentleness not usually associated with admirals.

'You've had a busy forenoon, Gamble. How did your SAR trip end up?'

'DOA, sir.' Hob said.

'DOA?'

'Dead on arrival.'

As so often occurred in the SAR squadron, the satisfaction of skilful flying was too often marred by tragedy. The crews were hardened men but the deaths of children affected even these professionals.

'What sort of casualty?' the admiral asked quietly.

'A six-year-old girl, sir. Her dog's okay.'

There was silence at the other end. Hob added: 'There's the Dodman coming up, sir. Fine on the port side.'

'814 Squadron is joining *Furious* tonight,' the First Sea Lord said. 'Hunting Soviet submarines will be more to your taste, I suspect.'

'Yes, sir.' Hob glanced sideways at his second pilot: 'Your lever,' he commanded. He would relax for a few minutes before taking the chopper across the Sound.

Funny how life dealt the cards. This early morning had been good news; he could see Allie now, standing in the porch while she waved him off. Her face had been radiant.

'Dodman abeam to port,' the observer chipped in from the back.

Hob glanced down at the surging rollers of the confused sea which always built up here on the ebb, then the milkiness of St Austell Bay came up and the entrance to Fowey. Minutes later, Polperro appeared, where, a fortnight ago, Allie and he had whiled away a Sunday, happy in the driving rain as they tramped the cliffs towards Lantivet. They loved the place and the cider was good.

'My lever,' Hob said, as the dark bluff of Rame Head grew in size.

'Your lever.'

'You'll see the Sound at any minute, sir,' Hob reported to his passenger. 'We'll be landing in five minutes.'

'All ready in the back,' the observer reported. 'Harnesses checked.'

The landing drill continued until the cliffs of Rame were sliding beneath the cab. Hob had decided to follow the shoreline and take her in over Cawsand and Torpoint. Already he could see the blue waters of the Sound. The observer was getting through to the dockyard heliport: 1200 exactly, and Hob could begin his approach procedures.

'Your harness secured, sir?'

'Secured.'

The curve of Cawsand Bay slid beneath them. Drake's Island came abeam to starboard and then, as Hob turned to put Torpoint on his port bow, the sprawl of Devonport opened ahead. He steadied 827 on the three covered dry docks of the frigate complex; he identified the nuclear submarine refuelling and refitting base on the Hamoaze, where there seemed to be much coming and going along the perimeter road.

'Stand-by, sir –'

But Hob, who had begun to lose height, never finished his sentence. As he peered downwards, a blinding light streaked across his vision. Then, just clear of the frigate complex, a turmoil of brown dust and smoke, an orange fireball flashing at its core, jerked skywards. More explosions flickered ahead of him as the first of the shockwaves blasted Sea King 827, slamming her bodily sideways. Hob allowed her to fall from the sky, his fingers poised above the collective, ready to counter the uncontrollable antics as soon as the turbulence ceased. He counted eight shocks, before he halted his helicopter. The frigate complex ahead of him and half the town of Devonport beyond the dockyard wall had erupted into a cauldron of fire and swirling brown smoke.

'I'm putting her down, sir,' Hob announced sharply. In a few seconds, the helicopter pad would be obliterated by the dust clouds from the collapsing buildings.

4

Devonport, 12 April. Last night, when she had finally shut the door of the spare room on him, Gwen had told Ozzie that there would be no lie-in for either of them – and she had been dead right. She devoted her Saturday mornings to giving a thorough going-over of her new home, 17 Cunningham Street. She was having to work full time after her husband, Niv Fane, died in the *Icarus* incident, but today, if Oz could help her by doing the shopping, she could farm off the children to her parents for the afternoon and evening.

Thomas Osgood, now Leading Aircrewman Osgood, whistled as he closed the gate behind him, that drawbridge protecting Gwen and him from the realities of existence. Since Niv's death she had withdrawn inside herself; however gently her neighbours tried to settle her into this new neighbourhood, she still kept up the barriers.

Osgood pulled up the collar of his blue anorak and squared his cap firmly. The *Seahawk* cap ribbon was respected in Devonport and gave a man a head start over those still sporting the *Drake* emblem – but he was still self-conscious about wearing his DSM. The northerly wind cut through him as it whistled down the street from off the moors. The shopping-bag swung from his hand as he strode down the hill: walking to the supermarket would give Gwen more time.

It seemed three years, not three months, since his survivor's leave. The only other *Icarus* man whom he bumped into was Lieutenant Gamble, the Lynx pilot who had encouraged him to transfer to the Fleet Air Arm. The pilot had been pleased to see him, and had already heard of Osgood's winning his wings as a newly-fledged aircrewman.

The going had been tough – the training of an aircrewman in peacetime took almost six months, but the *Icarus* incident had jolted the Navy on to a war footing. By cutting out some of the less important ingredients in the training, an aircrewman now completed the course in three months. Under these wartime conditions Culdrose was concentrating on only the tactical essentials: winch operation and general aircrewmanship. Then one had to choose – SAR missile aimer, 'Junglie' (working with the Royal Marine Commandos) or ASW sonar operator. Osgood had not regretted opting for the latter – the impending battle in the Atlantic might be becoming hot at any moment. The Navy's task would be to sink every Soviet submarine it could.

He had enjoyed his course, particularly the last few weeks spent in 706 Squadron where the training became relevant for the first time. After the Portland training he had become part of the team, hunting ping-running submarines in the exercise areas of the Western Approaches.

For the first time, he felt that he was personally affecting events: the success or failure of a submarine hunt depended upon his and the observer's skill. The aircrewman was an indispensable member of the front-line team. The chopper boys competed with the submariners as the *crème de la crème* of the Royal Navy.

'Hi, Oz!'

Turning into the doors of the supermarket, Osgood bumped into one of the maintainers with whom he had ganged up at Culdrose. The man was grinning as he awkwardly introduced the blonde clinging to his sleeve.

'Heard the buzz, Oz?'

Osgood shook his head cautiously.

'Our PO reckoned there'd be a general recall after this morning's news.'

'Bulgarians going into Turkey?'

'S'right, and the PO said we'd better check up with our authorities.'

'Have you been through yet?' Oz asked. 'To *Seahawk*?'

'Too busy,' the sailor said. He winked and the girl giggled. 'See you, Oz,' and the maintainer merged with the stream of shoppers shuffling from the store.

Osgood loathed supermarkets, especially on Saturday mornings. But then, he'd been lucky to get this weekend: he was escaping the bull of an admiral's inspection, but he ought to ring the base after this morning's news. At least he could share this afternoon with Gwen. The memory of the misery he had experienced during those first days of his survivor's leave was still like a knife-thrust in his guts. He had paid a last visit to the flat in Roborough where his wife, Merle, had left him, taking their daughter with her. But new tenants were already installed and he had slunk away, undecided whether to get drunk or to find his way back to barracks. He had tried to put Gwen Fane out of his mind, for he hadn't heard from her since he had handed her the ring which they'd prised from Niv's finger. He still felt embarrassed when he remembered breaking down in front of her. She had just been widowed and needed strength as much as he did – but it was she who had been rock-like, offering her friendship, if ever he needed it.

So he had decided to track her down during his survivor's leave, and found her in her new home, a Victorian semi in Cunningham Street. It was, he supposed, their loneliness and unhappiness which had drawn Gwen and him together. During those first days, their need for comfort and reassurance had been mutual and unspoken. But as the weeks went by and their caution wore off, their friendship became more natural. Neither had asked for much, yet slowly they had become very fond of each other. He admitted to himself, now, that he had always intended to see Gwen again. Last night, for the first time, they had tentatively discussed the future, a tomorrow beset by the imminence of war; it was she who had hinted that life might be better if they could share it. Gwen was a mature woman in comparison with Merle and she had a mysterious attraction to which he could put no words. How he wanted her now, a thousand times more than he had lusted for Merle.

He tossed the loaves of sliced bread on top of the trolley and joined the supermarket pay queue. He'd be lucky to get back to Gwen before midday – bloody hell – and this might be their last afternoon together for months. Why, for Pete's sake, shouldn't he ask her to marry him? Stupider things had been done before. He knew now, during those long evenings in the mess, that life was bloody without her. Perhaps, if she wouldn't marry him, she might live with him? But no, he knew without asking that only marriage would do. . . . Suddenly he heard the loud speakers blaring an announcement above the shoppers' heads. The manager was telling them that the Prime Minister would be on television at one o'clock. There was a moment's silence and then some wag shouted something Osgood could not hear. There was a ripple of laughter around the store. At last it was his turn. He paid up and left the place, the shopping-bag in one hand and a bulging carton tucked beneath his other arm.

It was 1150 when the bus put him down at Armada Close. There was time for a pint across the road at the Admiral Bruce Fraser and he could call *Seahawk* from there. As he crossed the road, he caught sight of the red telephone-box standing on its own at the corner. Osgood set the shopping against the metal frame of the door and pushed his way inside. Three minutes later he was through to the regulating office at Culdrose.

'Leading Aircrewman Osgood? Yes. You're right – general recall. Report back to base immediately . . . got it?'

'Yes, Chief.'

He put down the receiver. Bloody hell. . . . As he turned for the door a violent shock blasted his ears; and then there was the roar of a gigantic explosion from the direction of the dockyard. It was followed by another, then another, each nearer than the last. He stood transfixed, waiting. Instinctively he shoved his back against the door of the booth when a stunning explosion erupted about him. He heard the shattering glass, felt the pain in his ears and the searing heat. He grabbed at the ledge of the coin box. The world was spinning and he heard a roaring like an express train in a tunnel . . . and then he blacked out.

As Osgood's senses returned, he tried to focus, looking up from a settee in the lounge bar of the pub. The stench of stale beer made his nausea worse. The features of a grey and puffy face came together slowly, the anxious face of the publican gazing down at him. From far away Oz heard the conversation, though he had difficulty understanding.

'Okay, mate, there's no use trying the phone. Look – he's coming round. He's a tough bastard . . .'

Osgood heard the ambulances, the shrill of police whistles and the blaring car-horns. He could smell burning and, as he clambered to his feet and staggered to the door, he heard the publican yelling after him:

'You're safer in here, Jack. Come down to the cellar, with the others . . .'

But Osgood pushed open the swing doors and vomited into the gutter. Holding his splitting head, he localized the pain where his skull had cracked against the cast iron of the booth. He was sick again and then started blindly staggering towards the telephone-box, obsessively searching for his groceries.

The red booth was tilted on its side, his purchases spilled across the pavement. As he looked up to identify his way back to Cunningham Street, he saw the clear blue sky, blackened by billowing clouds of brown and orange smoke. Where there should have been houses there was nothing but space between the outlines of jagged masonry and drunken, leaning walls which were collapsing irregularly to the ground. From not far away he heard the screams of trapped people, crushed beneath the tons of rubble. High up in a half-demolished block, a woman clung, screaming dementedly, clutching a baby in one arm, a child in the other. As he watched, the structure slowly crumbled beneath her. The dust shot skywards, the horror of it mercifully obliterated by a cloud of swirling smoke.

Gwen . . . he knew now the meaning of blind terror. As he stumbled across the heaps of masonry, towards what must have been Cunningham Street, there was only one thought in his distraught mind: he had to reach her, to identify the house, though it might be only a hole in the ground. He shouted, 'Gwen! Gwen!' and searched frenziedly in the rubble for what might once have been her street.

A couple of policemen, their uniforms streaked by filth and dust, grabbed his arms. 'This area's out of bounds. Can't you read the notices on the barriers, mate?'

In spite of his struggling, they were gentle with him, firmly sending him on his way: 'Inquire at the emergency centre. They'll be the first to know.'

But it was hopeless: nothing but a smouldering, barren wilderness. A sullen anger began seething inside him, displacing the numbed despair, as he staggered, half-running, towards the main road. He was gasping for breath when he finally reached a trail of cars crawling towards Saltash Bridge.

5

Mount's Bay, 12 April. Trevellion was watching the transit of the tower behind Gulval steadying against the western edge of St Michael's Mount. In a depth of twenty-two metres HMS *Furious* was now within the lee of Land's End – and the transit protected him from any further easting. He turned from his position against the for'd windows of the aircraft-carrier's bridge and called across to Jasper Craddock, his Commander, Air in Flyco, the flying control position protruding from the port after end of the bridge:

'Carry on, Wings. 814 Squadron can begin embarking.'

'Right, sir. I'm getting in the engineers' stores first.'

Captain Pascoe Trevellion, DSC, turned to his navigation officer. 'Keep her within these limits, Pilot.'

'Aye, aye, sir.'

Trevellion took a final look through the windows, before leaving his bridge. It was 1740 and the sun, a hazy, crimson orb, was already merging into the murkiness hanging like a shroud over the Cornish coast. He did not like the look of it and the barometer was falling steadily. He extracted his tobacco pouch from his hip pocket and began filling his battered pipe. Twelve miles to the north-east, on the other side of Carrick Roads, Rowena Trevellion was going about her chores and preparing supper for Ben. She too must be thinking about the Prime Minister's broadcast...

So it *was* war, after all the pussy-footing and the frenetic contortions by a few of the Nato countries to buy peace at any price. But the alliance had stood the strain – and the enemy attack on Plymouth would consolidate those loyalties. Martial law was being declared in the city, after the looting following the bombardment by an unidentified attacker – though Trevellion realized from the classified signal he had received this evening that the perpetrator of the outrage was probably the Echo II which CINCCHAN had sunk off Bishop

Rock – possibly the sub. contact which the minesweeper had picked up.

The commander, John Bellairs, an ex-submariner, heavily built and with a sense of humour, came up quietly behind him. 'Ship's darkened,' he said. 'First time for real, sir.'

'I wonder, John, how many nights it will be before the lights go on again,' Trevellion said. 'Our lords and masters think it will be over in a few weeks.'

'Let's hope they're right, sir: war has a funny habit of not going the way you expect.'

The captain was poking his finger at the armoured plate-glass window before him: 'Here they come – the first of the Wessexes.'

The red lights of the helicopters were blinking in an endless string from across the cliff tops, as they homed in on the carrier.

'The last of the draft are being brought off by the Scillies ferry from Penzance, sir. I've lowered the port gangway.'

Trevellion drew in upon the tobacco as the bowl of his pipe flamed to his match. He snuffed out the flame. 'Can't do that any more,' he grumbled. 'Rotten example I'm setting, John,' and he grinned at his second-in-command. 'Is the ship's company complete?'

'Only two absentees, sir. All the Culdrose team made it, in spite of the Plymouth blitz.'

'Good. We'd better wear our Mae Wests from now on.'

'Right, sir. I've warned the ship's company.'

'Thank heavens we got the Harriers stowed when we did,' Trevellion went on. 'The trials finished only just in time.'

'The operational readiness inspection couldn't have been better timed, sir.'

Trevellion didn't answer, his thoughts ranging over those months now behind him. He had been pleased by the chance of commanding this ship: a senior captain, he had been in the right place at the right time when his predecessor had been invalided out. Perhaps the Admiralty had decided that *Furious* should be commanded by an officer who had suffered the first shock of war to show the Russians that the British meant business?

'I've organized a mail, sir, if you've got anything.'

'Thanks, John. I'll give it to my steward, if I have time to write.'

Trevellion was alone again with his thoughts, while the sun merged with the darkening horizon above Land's End. He felt cold and tired after this long day, his spirit at a low ebb. For all these weeks the free world had tried to postpone this awful event. From the moment last month when the Soviet Northern Fleet sailed west from the Barents, he had known that Armageddon was approaching. Two days ago, the US president had told the Kremlin that the sailings of the reinforcement convoys for Europe were imminent; he had also made it plain that any Soviet submarine interfering with these convoys would be sunk, and that the submarine bases from which they operated would be attacked. The corollary presumed to apply to Russian surface forces was obvious.

The Soviets had retaliated by attacking Plymouth. If the Kremlin thought that an act of such ruthlessness would weaken British will, it was making a profound mistake, one which had been made before. It was already clear from the radio and television newsflashes that the Plymouth atrocity was welding the British nation together, unifying the people as for World War II – and Trevellion breathed a prayer of thankfulness that out of chaos, providence had created once again a national leader with the capacity to unite the people and to fire them with the will to resist – to the end, if need be.

Nato's immediate retaliatory attack by the RAF and Royal Norwegian Air Force low-level fighter-bombers on Polyarnyy, the submarine base in the Kola inlet, had demonstrated the West's resolution. Losses had been devastating – only two aircraft from the two squadrons had returned to base. It would be some time before the results of the raid could be known, but for three hours there had been no more raids on land targets from either side.

The difficulty in attacking Polyarnyy lay in the use of weapons: the two British SSBNs on patrol were capable only of nuclear attack, and the Soviet onslaught against Plymouth had been with high explosive. The only American submarine-launched missiles fitted with HE warheads were Harpoons, which had a range of sixty miles – too short to fire from inside

36

Norwegian waters, even if the Russians were not occupying Nordland. And for a submarine to approach within forty miles of the Karelian coast, where the waters were shallow, presumably thickly mined and constantly patrolled, was an unrealistic proposition. The Tomahawk, the long-range submarine-launched cruise missile was undoubtedly standing-by in the wings if the gallant attack by the RAF and RNAF proved to have been fruitless.

The admiral's flag-lieutenant and personal pilot saluted behind him. 'Excuse me, sir: the admiral wonders whether you would join him for supper in his sea-cabin when you've finished on the bridge?'

'Thanks, Flags. About ten minutes.'

The flag-captain's eyes searched the horizon, checking once again. The scene was one of frenzied activity as the airlift from Culdrose swung into its stride. The Fleet Air Arm's headquarters at Yeovilton had flung in every available aircraft to complete this risky operation as swiftly as possible. Thank God, it was a night evolution, though darkness made the task trickier for the helicopter crews.

Flying the flag of Force Q's ASW Group Commander, *Furious* was one of Nato's few and valuable CAHs and therefore vital to the protection of Atlantic sea lanes: she must be presumed a high value target for the enemy in this imminent Atlantic battle. Trevellion considered that, even if the less important store items had not been embarked, he must take *Furious* clear of the Western Approaches before dawn: all the evidence pointed to enemy submarines in the offing. *Furious*' escorts, the Nato destroyers and frigates, were out there in the gathering darkness, patrolling to seaward to guard Mother. Trevellion pursed his lips – he knew what a frigate's life was all about.

'I'll be in the admiral's sea-cabin,' he said, nodding at the senior watchkeeper.

He walked aft to his sea-cabin at the back of the bridge and whirred the razor over his face: he had to stoop for the mirror and was startled by the haggard face staring back at him. Semi-circles of tiredness sagged beneath his clear, grey eyes. And now, with weariness evident after the intensity of these weeks working up his ship, his gaunt face, with its hooked nose and protuberant cheek bones, was more drawn than ever: it was not surprising that the troops called him 'Old Chough'. But the Cornish chough was a canny bird, and had a remarkable knack of survival. Trevellion was over six feet two and, having boxed and played rugger for the United Services in his youth, he sensed, when visiting the wardroom and messdecks, that his demeanour bred a certain respect. He smoothed down his thinning, greying hair and crossed the flat towards the ASW Group Commander's cabin where Rear-Admiral Roderick Druce, AFC, was awaiting him. Rear-Admiral Boyd, Flag Officer Carriers and COMSTRIGRUTWO, was stuck somewhere in the Norwegian Sea.

'Come in, Pascoe,' the ebullient voice invited. The admiral swept his hand towards the other chair. 'Gin? No, you don't, do you?'

'I could do with some squash, sir.'

Trevellion felt the moment of incredulity and faint embarrassment, but he had become used to the reaction over the years. 'Mind if I smoke?'

Roderick Druce was a caricaturist's dream: bushy, black eyebrows and a plump, double-chinned, jovial face, with dark brown eyes alive with humour. Trevellion liked this rollicking admiral whose enthusiasm infected men wherever he went.

'I thought we could go through things, Pascoe, before we get under way: you'll be needing sleep before the last of your Sea Kings is embarked.' The steward, who had been hovering in the background, drew the curtain across the doorway. 'About half an hour,' Druce called to him. 'The captain's joining me for supper.' He faced Trevellion and raised his glass. 'Good hunting, Pascoe.'

Trevellion smiled. 'Same to you, sir, and many of 'em.' But he felt the falseness of the traditional attitude before the blood and guts were spilled. Unadulterated horror awaited them in those vast, heaving wastes across which the first convoys would be sailing within the next few hours.

'D'ye hear the PM's speech?'

'No, sir. I was off the Smalls at the time.'

'Very good, I thought. Put the choice simply and succinctly. Since Afghanistan, we have woken up to the reality of the Soviet threat and we won't let them get away with their occupation of Northern Norway. The PM presented the Russian arguments which don't bear scrutiny: they've made it plain that we can never win a long war in Europe, because we can't reinforce our Nato armies. But to prevent these reinforcements from reaching Europe, the Russian Fleet will first have to win several sea battles in the Med, the Indian Ocean and of course the one that really counts.' The Atlantic was an hour's steaming from where *Furious* now gyrated.

Trevellion downed his drink in one gulp. The admiral pulled down the world map on the bulkhead.

'There, the Med. I've just heard that the Turks have totally mined the Dardanelles and the Bosporus. They're on a war footing and fighting fiercely, but it's all too late. The Black Sea Fleet slipped weeks ago into the Eastern Med.'

'Where's the Yanks' Sixth Fleet, sir?'

'In the Western Basin, blocking the Straits where Flag Officer Gib's minelayers are busy. The Soviet Mediterranean Fleet will have to fight its way out to reach the Atlantic.'

'It's after the Carrier Striking Force, sir.'

Druce nodded. 'The Russians are hard pushed in the Gulf area. The American mobile force hasn't been wasting time. As you know, their base at Berbera, which the Russians had conveniently built for them, is only 170 miles across the Red Sea from Aden; Djibouti, 140; and their Kenya base is only two days steaming from Socotra.'

'The Russian base at Tamridah?'

'A hot seat, I'd reckon, if I happened to be a Soviet commanding officer in that area. And Oman, with its American island base of Masiran still uncompleted, can watch the Strait of Hormuz as easily as the rock apes can goof across the Straits of Gibraltar. Hormuz isn't much wider.'

'Afghanistan was the biggest mistake the Russians ever made, sir.'

'I'm not so sure – but they were surprised at the speed which a nation they considered degenerate could unite to face the challenge.'

'Not so sure, sir?'

'I think the Kremlin calculated the political effects of their invasion of Afghanistan down to the last detail. The threat to our Gulf oil has diverted considerable American naval effort from the Atlantic.'

In the silence, Trevellion could hear the background scream of jet engines and the flutter of rotors as the helicopters arrived and departed across the darkened flight deck, less than twenty yards outside.

'The Kremlin reckoned that the crisis would evaporate with time,' Trevellion said, 'like Hungary and Czechoslovakia. But the Soviets have the Third World to contend with now – and India and Pakistan have a lot of Moslems too.'

'At least, we know where we stand,' Druce said. 'This gentlemen's agreement to knock hell out of each other at sea makes good sense. Hopefully, things will remain static on the central European plain until we see how things are going.'

'If the Kremlin and the Pentagon manage to keep control of events, sir.'

'Let's get down to it, Pascoe,' and Druce shoved the sailing orders across the table. 'To ensure the safe and timely arrival of the convoy . . . where've I heard that before?' He chuckled. 'At least we haven't been so damn silly as to heed the argument that independently routed ships will be safer.' He spread the chart of the Atlantic Ocean across his bunk. 'Sorry about this, Pascoe,' he said. 'I'll go through the orders broadly; my staff can give us the details afterwards.'

'The Canucs, sir, I understand?'

'Yes. The Canadians have always accepted Norway as their responsibility. This convoy, HX-OS 1, sails from Halifax at midnight tonight, Nova Scotia time, for Oslo. Eighteen ships, modern and all capable of twenty-six knots, carrying the Canadian Division and its equipment. Oslo will be ready for speedy unloading and disembarkment from 19 April onwards.'

'Northabout, sir?'

'Yes.' Druce smiled ruefully. 'I'm sorry, Pascoe, we haven't been able to brief you earlier but it was difficult enough getting my staff and me here. Planning Linchpin's been quite a headache . . .' He chuckled again as he pored over the chart, his stubby finger prodding at the vast ocean.

'The Soviet Northern Fleet has been poised here, north of Jan

Mayen island for some time now. It can push south through any of the gaps where our submarines are waiting. The Kremlin were on the hot line two hours ago telling the us President that ships of any nationality will be attacked if sailing in an Allied convoy – or even, if independently routed, they are carrying cargoes for Nato nations.'

'That ought to encourage the fence-sitters,' Pascoe said.

But Druce was tracing out the convoys' routes, their tracks a network of converging black lines towards the Western and Northern Approaches of the British Isles.

'Unloading at the ports may be as difficult as fighting through the convoy,' the admiral said. 'The Dutch are using troops at Europort: labour troubles can close the port as effectively as a hundred per cent mining operation.'

'There's not much point in delivering the convoys if we can't unload 'em,' Trevellion added, as he perused the plans. The Mediterranean convoys CH-MA 6 and CH-GE 7, from Charleston to Marseilles and Genoa respectively, were the only others sailing tomorrow. BO-EU 2, Boston to Rotterdam Europort was sailing on 14 April; and NY-AN 5, New York to Antwerp on 16 April. The English Channel would be crowded from 21 April onwards, if the convoys were fought through successfully.

Druce touched the red circle six hundred miles east of Newfoundland. 'Our rendezvous position with HX-OS,' he said, 'midnight, Monday, 14 April – your mean speed of advance is twenty-four knots, if you can sail within the next five hours.' He looked at his flag captain. 'D'you think the old lady can make it, Pascoe?'

There was a tap on the door and Jasper Craddock, cap under his left arm, stood in the doorway:

'The airlift's going better than I hoped, sir,' he said, reporting to his captain. 'I hope to be accepting the first of the squadron shortly before midnight and should be ready to proceed by 0045, sir.' He turned towards the admiral: 'I don't know whether I'll be able to provide the screen, sir – visibility is shutting down.'

Trevellion climbed to his feet and drew back the curtain which was across the scuttle. 'What's it like west of Land's End?'

'Probably worse, sir, according to the met. officer.'

'Cancel the Sea Kings, Wings. We've got our full surface screen.' Trevellion turned to his admiral for approval.

'I agree, Pascoe.' He was still scrutinizing the chart hanging on the bulkhead. 'I'd prefer to use radar until we're clear of the Longships and take no risks with the squadron. Very shortly we'll be needing every aircraft which can fly.'

As Craddock stepped from the cabin, Druce's steward began lowering the dead-lights and screwing up the wing-nuts on the scuttles. 'Darken ship, sir,' he said quietly. 'Your supper's ready when you are, sir.'

'Thanks, Blair.'

'We can talk about the enemy threat while we're eating.' Druce rose from his chair and ushered his guest into the minute compartment adjacent to his sleeping cabin. 'This'll be your last peaceful meal for some time, Pascoe,' he said. 'Reckon you're going to be busy.'

6

HMS Furious, 13 April. 'I have the ship, Pilot.'

'You have the ship, sir.'

'Half-ahead together,' Captain Trevellion ordered. 'Fifteen knots.'

The old ship was still oil-fuel fired, turbine-driven and telegraph-controlled, but 'Old Fury', as the troops called her, had come into her own during these last years of her life. *Furious* had held things together while waiting interminably for the new through-deckers, *Invincible* and *Illustrious*, to be completed.

'Fifteen knots, sir. Course two-four-oh.'

The navigating officer was taking no risks in this deteriorating visibility and had proposed joining the traffic separation zone south of Wolf Rock, instead of cutting between the rock and Land's End. The captain raised his binoculars to peer through the treated windows which cast no reflections. He identified the blur of light from the quick-flashing buoy fine on their starboard bow and at 0140 he brought *Furious* round; then he picked up the alternating white-red flashes of Wolf Rock sliding down the starboard side.

'I'm going into the wings,' Trevellion said. 'You have the ship, Pilot.'

He was glad to leave the darkened bridge for a moment. The PPIs were giving an accurate position both of his ship and of the traffic streaming in both directions. Ahead of *Furious* was the screen, each ship navigating by radar in this foul weather – but, as soon as they were into the Atlantic, radio and radar silence would be imperative.

It was cold out here in the wings. A bank of fog suddenly shrouded the ship, curling across the lip of the flight deck, so that he could not see her great bows.

'Reduce to eight knots,' he sang out over his shoulder. 'Double up the lookouts, Officer of the Watch. Start the foghorn.'

He knew that the young seamen could add little to the safety of the ship, but it would bring home to everyone that each man counted now. He would talk to the ship's company tomorrow at dinner-time, to put them in the picture. By then he should know more himself, though Roderick Druce had given him an up-to-date résumé at supper...

The long blast of the foghorn boomed suddenly above his head, its resonance making his eardrums vibrate. Then, as suddenly as the bank had descended, the ship broke through to clear weather and he stopped the horn. The red bow-light and the white steaming-lights of a big tanker slid down the other lane. He heard the melancholy wail of the diaphone from the Seven Stones. He shivered as the wind got up: a miserable, cold mizzle was superseding the patchy fog. It was 0340 already.

As he heard the blast from the horn of the Longships, away to the eastward, he sighted a patch of white light, fine on his starboard bow and on the edge of the northbound lane. The bearing was changing rapidly and even before he lifted his binoculars, he recognized a side-trawler. She was busy hauling her trawl and her string of white lights gleamed in the black water, the myriads of sea birds wheeling, a shimmering white cloud in the pool of light, as the 'side-winder' slid down the starboard side. To the north, a suspicion of twilight was showing, a faint lightening behind the night clouds strung above the horizon ahead. It was still dark in this dangerous bottleneck but, as soon as the carrier was clear and, provided the vis. held, he would fly-off his Sea Kings...

He could just pick out the smudge of the aging *Phoebe*'s outline, four miles to the northward. She and *Brazen* were the point-defence ships, their job being to shoot down with their Sea Cat and Sea Wolf missiles any aircraft which penetrated the area defences put up by the air defence ship, HMS *Gloucester*. The Type 42 destroyer could cover the whole force with her Sea Darts, providing her supply of missiles was adequate and that her re-loading drill was slick enough. Both she and FGN *Köln*, the Type 22 German frigate, were invisible in the night; and somewhere miles ahead, steaming westwards (and no doubt hoping that the carrier would soon catch up on her) was the heart of the whole force: *Oileus*, the Dutch fast combat support ship, who previously had been with STANAVFORLANT when Trevellion had commanded *Icarus*. *Oileus* was a fine ship, relatively modern and purpose-built. An improved Poolster, she could make twenty-one knots and, with sonar, two Sea Kings and three Lynxes, she could screen herself against submarine attack. A pity we had not been able to build similar ships, Trevellion thought gloomily. The British contribution, though manned by an excellent crew of Royal Fleet Auxiliary officers and men, was the obsolescent *Resolve*, capable of only sixteen knots. Now carrying weapons and ammunition, she had to be diverted up the Irish Sea to wait for the arrival of HX-OS 1 off Northern Ireland... Feeling the chill as first light dawned, Trevellion moved back into the bridge.

'Coming on to the clearing bearing,' the navigating officer reported. 'New course, 263°, sir.'

'Bring her round. Start the zig on an MLA of 263°. Increase to twenty-four knots.'

The carrier swung to her rhumb-line course which would take her to her rendezvous with the Canadian convoy. Spread around the lightening horizon, the grey smudges of Force Q's escorts were beginning to show up. Far ahead above the horizon line, the pinhead of *Oileus*' masthead showed intermittently as the carrier began to plunge rhythmically into the Atlantic swell. Trevellion strode a few yards to the Flyco bridge where Craddock was supervising the first flights of the day.

'Better get them off as soon as you can, Wings. The wind's blowing the dirt away.'

'Aye, aye, sir.' Craddock turned in his chair and nodded to Little F, the flying lieutenant-commander in charge of the flying details.

Trevellion felt reassured by his airmen. The team was by no means perfect yet, but the next few weeks would bring things up to scratch. Of one thing he was sure: Jasper Craddock was a ruthless Commander, Air, tough and demanding. Only time would show what his aircrews were made of; the result of the coming struggle depended upon these young men already assembling on the flight deck. So be it, Trevellion thought. The Russians had their objectives: to destroy our shipping and to sink our warships. But Nato, the US navy and the Royal Navy would give the Soviet Fleet such a bloody nose that it would be pleading for mercy before the agony was over. Trevellion handed the ship over to the officer of the watch and walked quietly from his bridge.

Trevellion was too experienced to be able to share the excitement of his officers. He well knew what these next weeks would be like; he was one of the few who had not only been in action but survived.

Outside the door of his sea-cabin, the communications officer confronted him with a signal: CINCCHAN had stumbled upon a field of complex enemy mines close to the Channel light vessel, where two British ships and a neutral had been sunk. All shipping was being diverted. From now onwards Force Q would be keeping radio and radar silence.

'Back to the Mark I eyeball,' he murmured as he initialled the message.

He pulled the curtain across the doorway (all doors had been landed during the last dockyard refit because of the jamming risk from sudden shock). He glanced at the photograph of Rowena, then heaved himself on to his bunk and turned on the dim lighting. For an instant, he jettisoned his awesome responsibilities – not only the safekeeping of his ship and a thousand officers and men but the safe arrival of this entire Canadian convoy depended upon *Furious* and her covering force. He turned wearily on his side and extracted a small Bible from the drawer under his bunk. The page fell open where it always did. His father's faded underlining of the passage was still just visible:

'Have I not commanded thee? Be strong and of a good courage; be not afraid, neither be thou dismayed: for the Lord thy God is with thee withersoever thou goest.'

Trevellion flipped shut the small book, replaced it beneath his bunk and snapped out the light.

7

HMS Furious, 13 April. The restrained atmosphere in the briefing room, Hob realized, was due not so much to the presence of the first eleven (Squadron CO, Little F and even Wings were already seated in the front row), but because of the news flooding in from all directions. It was now 0130 on Sunday, six hours after 814 Squadron had flown on, and no doubt remained: Soviet submarines had started attacking the convoys assembling off the American ports.

Hob, sitting in the second row, with his crew around him, shook his head: as senior pilot he had nothing to add to the briefing. He had done all he could to bring his pilots up to scratch and it was now up to them. He saw the ops officer glance at Wings, the redoubtable Jasper Craddock, whose jaw was jutting aggressively and whose obstinate mouth was set grimly, as if he was spoiling for a fight. Even if Craddock wasn't respected by everyone, as his predecessors had always been in 'Old Fury', he was certainly feared by his pilots. He was a driver impelled, some said, by ambition, because this was his last chance for promotion to captain. Craddock nodded: the ops officer opened the briefing by handing over to the duty met. officer.

The projector flicked on and the screen glared brightly in front of them, the weather forecasts for the next six and twenty-four hours demonstrated by the dark pressure lines heralding the lows and highs in their area and in the Atlantic. 'Force six, increasing to seven, perhaps gale eight,' the unemotional Welsh voice continued. 'The equinoctials, which didn't materialize at the end of March, seem to be late this year, judging by the lows building up in the western Atlantic and off Iceland: they could be more ferocious than usual.'

As Hob scribbled the essential details of the forecast on to the surface of his knee pad, Duggie Mann, the Squadron CO, stood up in the front row to address his fliers:

'Usual emergency procedures if you run into trouble,' he said. 'Stick with your aircraft if you can. Any questions?'

Hob raised his hand:

'May we break silence for maydays or for an emergency return to Mother, sir?'

'No. We're at war now.' The co added, a grin twitching the corners of his wide mouth: 'The homing beacons on your survival suits should get us to you.'

'The water's tropical down here,' the pilot of 819 contributed. '*Dolce vita* after North Cape.'

The duty pilot took over when Duggie Mann sat down. He looked up at the crew duty list and rattled off the chalked-in details:

'Advanced offensive Jez sweep: aircrafts 827 and 819; pilots Gamble and Trewby; crew, Gooch and Osgood; fuel, normal limits; armament, two Mark 46 torpedoes.' Hob was watching 819's Aircrewman Osgood, swathed in his flying gear, and smiled – there was someone who had shared those bloody awful moments in the Arctic seas. And, of course, it had been a proud moment when they had collected their gongs at the Palace with the other *Icarus* sailors.

Hob turned again to listen to the duty pilot repeating the communication details. The senior observer (SOBS) took over and Dunker Davies, Hob's observer, began scribbling down the navigational hazards, the diversions and the details of the radio aids. SOBS repeated *Oileus*' 0200 position, 160 miles ahead. 'Dip Boss will be SPLOT in 827. Usual Jumpex procedures. Mother will be maintaining her MLA and number five zigzag.' He glanced at the clock on the bulkhead and, as they checked their watches, he counted down the time. '0151,' he concluded, glancing at Wings, who climbed to his feet and addressed them all:

'The admiral wishes all senior officers in the ship to be updated with today's strategic and tactical situation,' he said briskly. 'His staff officer, operations would therefore like a word with the squadron's senior officers.' Craddock nodded at the aircrews sitting in the benches in front of him: 'Carry on,' he said. 'But I'd like SPLOT and SOBS to stand-fast, please. Flying stations in half an hour's time.'

No one had much to say as the crews climbed to their feet and picked up their bone-domes. Hob approached Osgood and shook his hand. 'See you when you get back.'

Osgood smiled briefly but said nothing, his brown eyes apprehensive. This was his first operational sortie – and this was war, not a Jez exercise from Culdrose. The crews filed silently from the briefing room.

'All yours, SOO,' Craddock said, as the grey-haired staff officer, operations took over the proceedings. The projector flipped and a new set of cards appeared on the screen:

'To start with, gentlemen, you all know that Rule of Engagement Number Three is in force – providing the target is identified as Soviet, you can shoot first. Alert State Red is now in force – we're most definitely at war.' A stencilled map of the Atlantic appeared on the screen and the pointer flipped from port to port, from one rendezvous position to another:

'Force Q's job is to cover Convoy HX-OS 1 which sailed from Halifax two hours ago. The others' – and his pointer touched the southern American ports – 'sail on the dates shown here. You'll notice that there is only one other sailing today, CH-MA 6 and CH-GE 7, from Charleston, a combined convoy which will separate after clearing the Straits of Gibraltar. The others sail on the fourteenth and sixteenth and by the beginning of next week congestion will be building up in the Channel ports.' He paused and displayed the next transparency:

'Here is Force Q at the moment, clearing west from Land's End,' and SOO tapped the circle marking the position of *Furious* at 0100. 'And here's *Oileus*, 164 miles ahead. She was allowed to press on ahead to gain time, remembering that she's only got a maximum cruising speed of twenty-one knots and could have held us back from our rendezvous with the convoy. But already things have changed rapidly, gentlemen,' and his pointer swept across two red arcs splayed west of the Fastnet Rock:

'Nimrod Bravo 2 has confirmed the general Sosus ellipse and has fixed two areas of enemy submarine concentration 220 and 400 miles to the west of us. This is obviously not an unexpected development but one which we must counter: *Oileus* is a high value target and is too vulnerable on her own, in spite of her own ASW capabilities.'

'Too bloody right,' Craddock muttered. 'The enemy are bound to know where she is.' Force Q, as they all realized, could not operate for long without her.

'Yes, sir,' SOO replied. 'The admiral is ordering *Oileus* to reverse course at 0400 and to rejoin the force. At the moment she's approaching the edge of the continental shelf and at 0400, when she doubles back towards us, she'll be eighty miles from the furthest-on position of Nimrod Bravo 2's confirmed sub – believed to be a Charlie. The signature isn't yet confirmed, but we can't rule out the risk of missile attack. *Brazen* is being sent on ahead to give *Oileus* point-defence cover. With a closing relative speed of forty knots, the FCSS should be joining us after dawn at about 0745. Until the frigate catches her up, we must give her ASW cover.'

SOO glanced at the Squadron CO, Duggie Mann. 'Attack any confirmed contacts,' he told him. 'Our own boats have been warned: our nearest submarine (one of the new Vickers' boats, *Upholder*) is ninety miles to the south-east. You can arm with Mark 46 torpedo warheads. Keep the Stingrays for the days ahead.'

'What about the other areas?' Duggie Mann responded. 'Any chance of our becoming embroiled with friendly forces or aircraft?'

The Atlantic chart flashed back on the screen.

'Identification has always been a big headache, as you know only too well,' SOO replied. 'Use IFF procedures if in any doubt, but not at the risk of alerting the enemy: we don't know how the battle will develop but these are the positions of our forces at this moment.' His pointer tapped the blue rectangles showing on the screen.

'Down here Nato's cheating a bit by positioning a task-force between the Canaries and Conakry to shield the fast VLCC convoy from the Gulf, PG-EU 8. You'll understand the reason in a moment, when I give you the rest of ACLANT's general intelligence situation.'

Hob was leaning forward, his chin in his hand, memorizing the array of forces.

'Our Striking Group One is patrolling there, south of the Azores; Carrier Striking Group Two is poised up here, north of

Iceland; and the main Carrier Striking Force is here off Greenland, 550 miles east-south-east of Cape Farewell.'

Whichever gap the Soviet Northern Fleet proposed to take, Hob realized, it would have to run the gauntlet; if the Soviets escalated the conflict to nuclear attack against American cities, retaliation would not come only from inter-continental ballistic missiles – carrier-borne strike aircraft could also pack a punch.

'. . . and there are several ASW forces covering the convoy lanes,' SOO continued, 'one down here, south-east of Charleston, another east of Norfolk; and, of course, our own Force Q which is rendezvousing here, nine hundred miles west of Newfoundland at midnight on Monday, tomorrow night.

'Now, gentlemen, let's look at the Soviet disposition, as known to us by today's general intelligence picture which is based on an assessment from all sources.' Sosus, the passive defence system depending upon hydrophones sited on the seabed, was one of Nato's vital defences. Positioned in the focal points of the Atlantic, these listening devices must be worrying the enemy submariner: not knowing whether or not his submarine was being tailed was unnerving for a submarine captain. Sosus and the passive helicopter sonobuoy were stripping the veil of invisibility from enemy submarine strategy . . . Hob's mind returned to the briefing – SOO was in full spate:

'Since the period of tension, the Soviet submarine fleet has taken up its war stations. These are today's dispositions . . .' His pointer traced the curved arcs ringing the focal points through which the West's convoys were compelled to pass. 'Twenty SSN fleet submarines here, straddling the convoy routes east of Charleston; forty SSNs twelve hundred miles to the eastward . . .' The Soviets had disposed two-thirds of their submarine fleet across the Atlantic lifelines, each boat separated by a minimum of a hundred miles from its neighbour – and, menacing the nodal points, the offensive patrol lines were doubled up, one 150 miles behind the other.

'Today's count totals 233 SSNs in the Northern Atlantic Ocean – I haven't included those in the Indian ocean, the Mediterranean and the North Sea where their patrol lines are disposed across the obvious sea lanes . . .' SOO's pointer lingered again on the red hatched arcs. 'Lying in wait for the Gulf convoys, a line of SSNs stretches west from the Cape Verdes and the Canaries. Three enemy major patrol lines, covering the eastern Atlantic seaboard of the United States, are orientated so that submarines can attack our convoys from most of the focal points: Panama, South America and Venezuela; the entrance to the Med; the bottle-neck to the Western Approaches, where the enemy's patrol lines are double-banked and through which our present track passes; and six patrol lines at least, A, B and C; P, L, and R, barring the Halifax–Arctic Gaps convoys.' The pointer drifted from the screen. No one spoke.

'The admiral has decided to charge straight through the present SSN threat across our track,' SOO concluded. 'He's requested COMSUBEASTLANT to withdraw his fleet submarines from our area for the next eight hours while we steam through.'

'We *can* attack any sub. contact?' Craddock asked.

'Yes, unrestricted between 10° and 20° west, and 48° and 51° north.'

'Where are the main surface units of the Northern Fleet?' Little F asked.

'If they're still north of Iceland, they're not in a very healthy position, are they?' Craddock added.

'Not since Carrier Striking Group Two reached its area east of Jan Mayen,' SOO agreed. 'Rear-Admiral Boyd, COMSTRIG-RUTWO, is steaming slowly eastwards, trying to tempt the Northern Fleet after him. There are signs that the feint is succeeding. The Northern Fleet turned east-north-east an hour ago and increased speed. Our Carrier Striking Force south of Iceland has begun to move north-east, to close the trap if the Northern Fleet turns nasty.'

'What about EW?' Craddock asked.

'Silent policy, except for enemy reports.'

'And the enemy?'

'He's been silent too: cat-and-mouse until recently, except that he's just started total jamming in the Iceland area, to protect his Northern Fleet, I imagine.'

Craddock nodded when the staff officer had switched off the projector. 'Now we can get on with the war.'

8

Sea King 827, 13 April. Hob hurried up to the air maintenance control room where 827's pilot, Grog Peterson, and the crews were waiting. Hob signed for his aircraft: all vital defects were made good. In the flat, they slipped on their bone domes, and fitted their throat mikes. Hob helped Dunker, a relatively inexperienced observer who had been paired off with Wally Gooch, an old hand at aircrewmanship. This practice was established now – sharing and balancing experience instead of manning selected aircraft totally with top-notch crews, as used to be the custom. They helped each other to adjust their survival packs slung about their backs; Dunker Davies leaned against the screen door. On the flight deck the wind buffeted their faces.

Hob sucked in his breath as the cold air hit them. The night was very dark, the vis. was right down, and it was blowing hard already. He hadn't flown on a night like this for months. He'd be relieved when this lot was over and he was again on board Mother, down below and deep in his pit. Bent against the wind whistling across the flight deck, they fought their way to spot 3 where 827 awaited them, rotors flicking in the eerie, violet sheen of the night lighting. There she crouched, that ponderous cab for which he now had a superstitious attachment. The handlers stood aside as the fresh crew floundered towards the doorways. The marshal raised his hand in greeting and Hob waved back.

Dunker was climbing in through the back door. He had plenty to do checking points as he took over from his predecessor, adjusting his seat, tightening the belts. Already fully briefed, he was immediately plotting Mother's position on the grid, laying off the course for the rendezvous with *Oileus*. He'd need all his skills tonight: there would be no help from Mother because of radio silence, a fact which made D, the flying director in the operations room, feel more than frustrated.

'Rotors running, refuelled and armed,' the exhausted but out-going pilot grinned happily, after they had plugged in their intercoms. 'Hope you enjoy it.' With his co-pilot, Grog Peterson, Hob began their vital actions:

'My lever,' he said quietly, once they had all checked communications through their bone domes.

'Your lever,' Grog acknowledged.

As Hob was reaching the end of his extensive list of checks, Dunker, the observer, piped up: 'Nearly ready in the back; Wally's just strapping in.'

Hob said: 'Am ready for STAB.' He could select either STAB, the stabilizing system, 'in' or 'out', depending on whether he wanted automatic or manual. He gave a thumbs-up to the marshal with the two illuminated batons glowing in his hands, whom Hob could see through the window. The batons lifted. Hob could test his STAB.

'STAB in,' Grog reported.

'Lifting,' Hob said. 'Torque coming in.'

He pulled in the lever to apply power; at the same instant, with his pedal he counteracted the tail rotor thrust, while he played with the cyclic – the forward and backward control – to lift the helicopter vertically from the deck: this was a critical operation, particularly as he was lifting off 'heavy', even in this wind. Grog was monitoring the instruments for the post take-off checks.

Hob lifted the machine upwards, then off to the left, towards the ship's side. Grog was peering left through his window to make sure his sky was clear, while Hob kept his eyes on the marshal – only he could warn the pilot if there was someone in the way or if something was going wrong ... if the marshal signalled 'hold', Hob had to obey. Hob applied power and took 827 across the darkened ship and away, climbing above the sparkling phosphoresence of her surging bow-waves. Dunker was calling over the intercom:

'Opening heading 263°.'

'Roger,' Hob acknowledged. '263°.'

As Hob climbed away, parallel to the ship in the inky blackness of the night, he pushed the nose forward and lifted her up, testing for the first time the maximum power on each engine.

He monitored the torque gauge while Grog checked the gas generator speed and the turbine inlet temperatures:

'Power good,' he said. 'Torque limiting 110 per cent. Standby for radalt,' he added.

Hob pushed her down to two hundred feet, but the sea was invisible beneath them. Grog checked that the two radar height channels were matched and then he plugged Hob into the radalt.

'Radalt coming in – now. Three, two, one,' Grog said. 'Radalt in.'

Hob felt the jolt.

'Bug moving,' Grog retorted.

The helo was now being controlled for height by the radar altimeter which was very accurate below two hundred feet; at this height the aircraft was flown automatically by the flight control system. Hob had no need to touch the collective – the lever which controlled the up-and-down motion – even if a gust caught her, because the system would automatically compensate.

Grog checked the lights. Off to starboard, Hob could distinguish 819's port light, their only visual link. It was lonely here in the dark cab on a black night, keeping radio silence. They carried out their pre-dip checks, so that they could go active at immediate notice. The sortie was up to Dunker now.

The observer had set up on his chart his position for latitude and longitude; and had also marked his grid position for easy reference. He would remain on his scale of five miles to the inch unless 827 became engaged in a hunt, when he would increase to one mile to the inch. He was sorting out his plot and trying to identify the other ships in the area, including *Furious* and her screen. He had picked up 819 and was signalling to her by lamp that he was ready to act as Dip Boss.

Wartime communications were very different from those in their peacetime exercises when radio chatter had made things so easy. With several enemy Charlie submarines ahead of the Force, to transmit would have been suicide for Mother. The chat had taken place at the briefing – each aircrew knew that both aircraft were armed with Serpents (their code word for the torpedoes) and that they had four and a half hours' endurance until 0500 – Charlie-time – the moment they had to quit the screen in order to regain the carrier.

'Okay in the back?' Hob asked.

'Yeah – nothing to do,' Dunker said. 'We should pick up *Oileus* at 0320. *Brazen* should be with her at 0430.'

They settled down to the long haul westwards. The wind seemed to be easing, but visibility at this height remained poor. Hob handed the cab over to Grog. It would have been easy, in the relative cosiness of the dimly-lit cockpit, where the only light came from the illuminated dials, to allow drowsiness to affect them, but tonight, for the first time in their lives, they were out on the hunt for real. They were here, ahead of 'Old Fury' to fight her through the enemy's encircling submarine force. *Furious* was steaming too fast to use her or the escorts' sonars, so her safety depended entirely upon her own helicopters.

The minutes slipped by and Hob jumped in the darkness when Dunker's voice cut in suddenly through the background scream of the vibrating machine.

'*Oileus* ought to be coming up soon, Hob.'

The time was 0252 and, as Hob took over his lever again, he heard the chatter of radio messages coming through to the observer.

'What's up, Dunker?' Hob asked as soon as there was a break.

'The policy's changed: hundred per cent radio and radar freedom,' the voice from the back said. 'Telebrief completed with Flyco. I'm through to D: he's coming in now . . .'

While the observer concentrated on the messages pouring through from D, the flying director in the ops room, Hob and Grog checked their electronic gear: it was good to be in touch with the world again on this dark night, reassuring to be able to use the radar and IFF. 819 was a couple of miles astern of station but was overhauling quickly: she too had got the buzz.

'Hob,' Dunker called, 'things are warming up. The sitrep gives fifteen SSNs between 47° and 50° north, disposed north-west, south-east. Nimrods have confirmed two SSNs, and possibly a third whose position is still not localized. The confirmed contacts are Charlies, one on each side of Mother's MLA, thirty-four miles from us and closing at speed. *Oileus* is reversing course to close Mother at full speed. They should meet at 0640, but *Brazen* is pushing on at full speed to join *Oileus* by 0500. *Brazen*'s Lynx is joining *Oileus*' Sea Kings who are screening her forty miles to the westward. They'll start pinging as soon as they're in position.'

'What about us?'

'Hold on – D's coming through . . .'

So, Hob thought, Rear-Admiral Roderick Druce had changed his mind. He was determined to fight his way through and, by blasting the area with active sonar transmissions from all sources to scare the daylights out of the attacking Charlies, which were torpedo-firing boats, though a missile attack could not be ruled out if the Nimrods' signature classifications were wrong.

'Hey, you up front . . .'

'Yep, Dunker?'

'819 and us and two of *Oileus*' Big Dippers are to form a Jez screen fifteen miles astern of her. We can attack any sub. contact immediately: normal procedures.' Then he was getting through to 819, in code, referring to *Oileus* as '*Clara*'.

'819, this is 827. Stand by to lay a Jez barrier. *Clara* seven miles decimal four.' The co-pilot was tracing his finger on the small display in the cockpit and Hob could distinctly see the blip of the replenishment ship.

'Take the cab up, Hob,' Dunker called. 'Fifteen hundred feet. *Oileus* is turning back now and I'm in contact. We'll pass over her and set up our Jez as soon as we pick up their Big Dippers.'

'Radalt out.'

Hob took her up while in the back Wally and Dunker prepared the sonobuoys.

'There she is.'

It was Grog who first saw her wash, a white snake in the black sea below. Dunker was on the air again, talking to 819 as their Dutch friends closed fast from the left:

'819, this is 827. Two Big Dippers joining ahead at fifteen hundred feet, one hundred knots. I carry two Serpents and we have no restrictions.'

Then Hob heard the guttural voices of the Dutchmen, and

when he glanced to port, he saw 849's and 850's red lights winking while the Dutch Sea Kings approached. He could see *Oileus* plainly, her ghostly outline rolling rhythmically while she ploughed before the south-westerly swell.

'Heading 268°,' Dunker ordered. 'Stand by to lay first Jez in eight minutes time.'

In the back, Dunker and Wally were still preparing the buoys and their plots. The 195 sonar body would be ready in a few minutes, all-set for immediate lowering if they had to go active. Dunker was on the line:

'Better be slick with the lay, Hob. Nimrod Uniform's just come up: Charlie number two's overhauling fast – doesn't seem to give a damn she's being tailed. She'll be within torpedo range of *Clara* in seventeen minutes, if she can get through our active screen.'

9

Sea King 827, 13 April. By 0325, as the grey twilight lightened
into dawn, 827 and 819 were carrying out their Jez routines five
miles astern of the FCSS, *Oileus*. In the back end of 827, the
aircrewman, Wally, was operating his Jez: concentrating over
his table, his pencil poised as he watched the frequency lines on
the roll of paper creeping across his plot, he was unusually
silent. The action astern of them had concentrated the minds of
everyone. Dunker, sitting in the observer's seat opposite the Jez
operator, was also glued to his sixteen-inch ground-stabilized
plot, a radar display angled up at 45° so that he could trace the
tracks of any target on to the display, which also served as a
plotting surface. His plot showed the true motion; not only did
he always know where he was relative to all other ships and
aircraft, but he could track the position of other helicopters and
ships in the screen as well as the courses and speeds of the
enemy.

'Okay, Hob, new heading 245°.'

Out to the westward, they listened to the action as *Oileus'* Sea
Kings, 849 and 850, and *Brazen*'s Lynx carried out the first kill.
The SSN had inexplicably committed suicide by continuing
dived at thirty-two knots towards *Oileus*. The chase had been
thrilling to overhear, but after the first involuntary cheer, the
silence after the torpedo kill had left the occupants of 827
stunned: the sound of the enemy's bulkheads exploding at
depth was not pleasant.

Hob and Grog had nothing to do up-front during a Jez sortie,
but today they would not carry out any practices. Hob was
up at fifteen hundred feet to get a better all-round view of the
field – the Jez operator had become used to *Oileus'* noise
and that of *Brazen* who was already in radar contact with
the Dutchman. It was at 0334 that 849 came up with the
doubtful frequency signature which alerted everyone ... but
it was quickly ignored after 819 had investigated along a track

59

of 077°. 849 must have been confused by *Oileus'* signature as the ship threshed eastwards towards the shelter of mother's approaching screen.

After the false alarm, *Brazen* streamed her foxer (an acoustic decoy), and *Oileus* followed her example. Distraught by the underwater racket, Wally was muttering filthy oaths at the back; Grog was still chuckling when the atmosphere became electric.

'I've got a frequency coming up,' Wally announced.

Hob looked down at the sea, now a steely grey. *Oileus* was pounding to the east; closing her was *Brazen*, a frigate of the Broadsword class whose sleek, functional lines plunged into the swell, the spume rising high above her bridge as she careered westwards.

'Okay,' Wally reported sharply from the back end, where he crouched over his Jez plot, facing the port side. 'Okay, I've got a target on buoy five.'

'Can you clarify?' the observer cut in.

'Yes – it's a Charlie.'

Things began moving fast. Dunker passed his data to the other helicopters, while Hob engaged down. The aircraft lunged forwards and began losing height as it swooped automatically to the dip position. Hob told Grog to monitor the height and the FCS authority, while he himself checked the altitude, air speed and the rate of descent.

Hob felt curiously remote as for the hundredth time he allowed the computers to take over. He deliberately released several of the systems in order to speed up the operation, taking over the cab manually for positioning and by allowing the FCS to find the hover height of forty feet. Then he would let the system catch up again and take over both height and aspect.

'*Christ!*' Grog rapped suddenly, peering through his port windows.

Hob caught sight of the faint torpedo tracks below them, two fingers streaking through the sombre waters. The leading fish was curving on its course, as it followed then closed in on *Oileus'* wake.

'Look, Hob – it's going for the foxer.'

They both saw the explosion, a huge circular, milky hump on

the surface when the sea erupted. A vast column of black and brown foam leaped hundreds of feet into the air. Hob could see *Oileus* sheering away to starboard, her captain obviously aware that the tracks had approached from the port quarter. No doubt her hooter was blowing, and she would be wasting no time in streaming her spare foxer.

'*Brazen*'s arrived just in time,' Hob said as, lightly monitoring the controls, he waited impatiently for the cab to lose height. 'Spot her foxer, Grog?'

'Yep – a long way astern.'

'Okay in the back?' Hob asked. 'There's a sub. there for sure ... Try to get through to *Brazen*, Dunker, and tell him to watch out. The sub.'s fired only two fish.' Hob could see the frigate, an impressive sight as she heeled to her emergency turn to port.

'Roger,' Dunker said. 'Get down in the dip soon, for God's sake, Hob.'

It seemed an eternity before the machine got them from ninety knots at two hundred feet to zero speed at forty feet. But then they were down, in the hover, the grey sea splashing white with the occasional, lazy wave. Hob and Grog checked that the cab was directly into the wind, as the doppler indicated by its crossed hairs.

'Heading two-six-oh,' Grog reported. 'I've got five knots on my ASI.'

'Five knots on ASI,' Hob said. He slid open his window for a final check. It was difficult now that the wind had died – he was having to use hundred per cent torque because they were fully loaded. 'If anything happens, we'll go in,' Hob said. 'No question about it: we're too heavy.'

'Right,' Grog said. The others in the back had also understood the message.

'Roger,' Dunker said. 'Okay for Wally, too.'

'Ts and Ps are all good,' Hob said, continuing the drill.

'Attitude?' Grog asked.

'Attitude – one degree nose up. Two degrees, left wing low.'

They checked the doppler and trimming, and the system took over ...

'First dip checks complete,' Hob reported. 'Lower the body.'

Dunker came in: 'Roger – lower the body. All round sweep, axis 270. High frequency scale eight.'

Then Wally reported: 'Fifty feet.'

Hob breathed a sigh of relief – the ball was well below the surface now and switched to 'cable hover', the device which took all the sting out of keeping the aircraft vertically over the ball. Once the computer sensed the slant on the cable it would manoeuvre the helicopter so that it was always vertical. If the cable began to drag, the sonar body would be tilted beyond limits and would no longer transmit.

The observer had taken a bathy reading. After all the recent weather there was little 'layer' trouble, the eternal problem caused by different temperature gradients. The ball could go down as deep as they wanted . . .

'One hundred feet,' Wally reported. 'We're sticking at that.'

Wally was now immediately alongside the observer's position. He was already pinging, starting at north and was sweeping round to west. He had transmitted three pings when Hob was nearly deafened inside his bone dome.

'*Whoops!*' Dunker yelled, unable to contain himself. 'Sonar contact, 290° – tracking, zero-four-zero.'

'Cripes! That was quick. Are you sure?' Hob queried.

Dunker: 'Okay. We'll have a look at it.'

'Buck up – not much time,' Hob said. 'What sort of confidence is it?'

'Definitely a sub. It's got two knots, opening doppler. Just losing it, Hob – fading. Transponder to code retain switch,' and Dunker was on the air telling the others that he was 'hot'.

'*Flash . . . flash . . . flash.* This is 827. Sonar contact 290° – range two zero, contact fading. 827 – out.'

The observer needed a couple of minutes of firm contact to achieve a plot – but he knew now that 819, 849 and 850 would be lifting their bodies and were preparing to join 827 . . . He was on to them again:

'827 – sonar contact: 295°; range one-five; tracking zero-four-five; speed six. 819, 849, 850 join me. Execute Plan Corral. *Over.*'

'Come on,' Hob snapped. 'Let's get the bastard before he fires the rest of his salvo.' Dunker was muttering from the back:

'Bloody hell,' he cried, 'the contact's fading. Prepare to jump.'

'Raise the body,' Hob snapped. '*Quick*.'

'Raising the body,' Wally replied. 'Seventy ... fifty feet.'

Grog switched over. 'Doppler,' he announced.

'Jump – 300°,' Dunker ordered. Hob was squinting over his shoulder at the aircrewman who was wrestling with the winch and body.

'Get that body in. *Get it in*.' Then he heard Wally shouting from aft:

'Body housed and latched.'

'Ready at the back,' Dunker snapped. 'Jump! Modified FCS, heading 300°.'

'Engage up,' Hob ordered.

'Engaged,' from Grog.

Again that interminable wait for the seventy-eight seconds while the FCS climbed them out of the hover to the exit speed at two hundred feet – but at sixty knots and at hundred feet Hob released the cyclic to give him pilot control. He turned her sharply right.

'Steady 300°. Transit checks, please.'

'Fuel Ts and Ps are all right,' Grog called. 'Oil temperature seems to have gone up a bit. I'll keep an eye on it.'

'Right: mark it.' Grog marked it with the chinagraph while he continued his monitoring: 'Rest of the Ts and Ps are good. Authority is good.'

Hob's nagging concern over the engine temperature was interrupted by Dunker at the back:

'Okay. Ready up front to go in?'

Hob said: 'Let's have a modified.' He could save a lot of time that way.

'Roger,' Dunker agreed. 'Stand-by to mark dip Right, modified, decelerate.'

Hob flared the cab back to sixty knots. As she dropped, he watched *Brazen* swinging in towards *Oileus*' wake, a superb sight, but she was getting in the way. As the cab pulled back, he put her into twenty degrees of bank and went straight into the hover.

'Transition,' the observer called.

'Engage down.'

They went through the drill again until Hob got them down to forty feet. He could see the sea, blue-grey now, churning in the whirls from the down-draught of the rotors.

'Authority's good,' Grog monitored. 'You're four up; you're three left; Ts and Ps are good.'

The body was already on its way down and Dunker was itching for Wally's first transmission. The ping whanged home.

'819, execute radar vectac.' Dunker, his voice tense, was vectoring the other *Furious* helicopter over the sub contact.

'Stand-by to drop serpent...' From the corner of his eye, Hob glimpsed *Brazen* in the middle of her emergency turn to starboard. She was heeling to her beam-ends while astern of her a huge wave humped in the frothing confusion of her wake.

'*Drop, drop, drop!*' Dunker was yelling to 819 who at two hundred feet was lunging into the attack. The glistening torpedo seemed to float downwards ... then Hob saw the splash where it parted the waters.

'Hob!' Grog shouted, deafening the earphones as he jabbed at the port window.

Then Hob saw the danger: *Brazen*'s foxer was directly below the cab. Four faint traces were streaking towards the decoy, four torpedoes in echelon, each packed with HE in its snout.

'*Cut the ball!*' Hob ordered. 'Hold tight.' He switched to manual and grabbed the collective. 'We're getting out.'

He felt the jolt when Wally fired the explosive cutter. The cab lurched to port, the first torpedo exploding as it homed on to the foxer beneath them. The helicopter was hurled upwards, caught at the edge of the pyramid of heaving water spouting skywards from the surface of the sea.

There was a shattering bang from aft. The tail had gone. Hob wrenched at the cyclic as the cab began gyrating downwards, out of control.

'*Brace ... brace ... brace...*' he yelled as he stiffened his muscles.

There was a pulverizing shock, thumping the breath from his lungs, as the machine crashed into the undulating swell. Dunker shouted from the back: 'Wally's hurt!' Grog was gasping too: he had been caught trying to get back into his seat, his

64

harness unlocked, as he leaned forwards to manipulate the controls.

Hob, a sharp pain in his back, realized that the cab was not, after all, turning upside down. He had been about to stop the engines and brake the rotors, but the cab was floating and appeared to be taking up a steep bow-up angle.

'Water's flooding in at the back,' Dunker yelled.

'Abandon!' Hob yelled. 'Get Wally out through the rear door.'

Hob felt Grog's boot on his shoulder as he thrust to escape through the port window.

'Door's open,' Dunker yelled. 'Wally's out.'

While Dunker followed the injured aircrewman into the heaving sea, Hob felt two distinct thuds. Then, a split second later, another rumbling explosion clanging against the bottom of the helicopter's hull. The cab heaved suddenly and wallowed uncontrollably as *Brazen*'s wash hit her. She was tilting backwards, pitching dangerously, until Hob feared for the rotor tips. He cut both engines and banged the explosive button for the flotation bags. He slipped his harness and was about to bash his elbow against his escape window, when it suddenly dawned on him that the cab was no longer sinking. Miraculously, she was still the right way up. The crew were clear and he was still alive. 'Panic not, Gamble,' he muttered to himself. 'Stay with the aircraft and you'll be all right.' He remained in his seat and waited.

Sea King 819 picked up Grog Peterson. 849 recovered the injured Wally and Dunker. Ten minutes later, Hob watched *Brazen* drifting down towards his stricken chopper. The pain in his back had eased and he climbed out to fix the slings. The machine was hauled from the water but was kept awash until it could be transferred to *Oileus*' big hoists. Balancing abaft the after slings, Hob saw 819 and 849 hovering not far distant and, etched against the horizon, the upperworks of *Furious*.

A bowline flopped across his shoulders and he was soon being hoisted up the sheer side of the wallowing frigate. They helped him across the scuppers and hauled him to his feet. Hob's back ached and he was trembling with cold. Someone supported him when he swayed for a moment, staggering against the rolling of the ship. His sodden clothes dripped and a pool of water formed slowly around his flying-boots.

A wardroom steward stepped forward, a shining tray balanced in his hand, his face bland:

'Ginger ale in your brandy, sir?'

The first lieutenant was waiting for Hob to down the neat spirit.

'I'll take you up to the captain.'

He led the way for'd along the iron deck. As they paused by the screen door, Hob paused to glance down again at his helicopter, a feeling of regret sweeping over him as he regarded his bent and twisted machine. He was surprised to see a spurt of white smoke puffing through the windows, followed by an orange glow, and then crimson tongues of flame. In seconds, an intense fire was raging from somewhere inside the stricken cab.

The seamen walked back on the recovery wire and dunked the helicopter back into the sea until the fire had burnt itself out...

After all he had done, the valuable Sea King was out of this war for a long time to come. Helped by the first lieutenant, Hob hauled himself slowly up to *Brazen*'s bridge to report to her captain. It was then that he remembered he had failed to ditch the pyrotechnics.

10

HMS Furious, 14 April. The man in the upper of the four bunks gave a cry, threshed with his legs until the screening curtain quivered, then uttered a long, despairing groan.

'For Pete's sake,' a voice in 4N8 mess blurted in exasperation from the bottom bunk in the dark corner. 'Belt up, Osgood.'

The dreamer in the top bunk was aware only of a distant cry from somewhere, far distant. He flung himself on to his other side to face the steel bulkhead. Sweating, he tossed the blanket from him, hearing briefly the background whirr of the fans and the huffing from the louvres in the ventilation trunking. Osgood sighed and tried to resist the images weaving through his tormented sleep...

Gwen's eyes were glistening marbles, the irises dark and pulsating with terror. Her brown hair was streaming behind her in the wind, and her mouth was parted as she 'gasped for breath. Stumbling, running, but never approaching closer, her hands reached out to him, the long fingers mutilated, the nails torn, oozing blood at the quicks. Behind her, clouds raced before the gales blowing across the Yelverton moors. A high rise tower block jerked suddenly – and he watched with horror as a zigzag crack developed, slowly at first, then faster, streaking up the sides of the tower until they reached the top. The monstrous building split wide, both sections toppling outwards. The roof collapsed, then slid, slowly at first, gathering momentum before crashing over the edge of the crumbling edifice. Slowly the two halves opened, curving like the flare in a carrier's bows; the sides seemed to float downwards in slow motion – and as the mass of rubble disintegrated into a billowing mushroom of dirt and dust, he heard Gwen's voice, small and shrill. Her image blurred and he couldn't distinguish her now from the others, multitudes of them, stumbling frenziedly as they ran – but the distance remained the same, never diminishing, though his lungs were bursting as he charged after them. He gasped out loud.

'...at 1630,' Osgood heard vaguely, as he surfaced from his nightmare, 'lower deck will be cleaned in half-an-hour's time.'

Osgood lay motionless, smelling the staleness of an over-crowded mess; he felt someone thump the side of his bunk.

'C'mon,' a voice croaked like a nutmeg grater. 'You're not in small ships now, Aircrewman Osgood.'

Osgood recognized the voice: Petty Officer Kotta, their divisional PO, was, as Osgood's messmates had already warned him, a bastard. 4N8, the leading hands' overflow mess since the squadron joined, was anathema to the PO. It was out of the way, too full of senior leading hands and other odds and sods. Osgood had sensed the rottenness of the mess from the moment he joined. He wiped the palm of his hand over his sticky face, glad to be free of his nightmare.

'Old Fury', as they called her, was somewhere to the west of Land's End; her ancient engines were pounding away, driving her towards her rendezvous with the convoy – Osgood still had no clear idea of the rendezvous position, though Toastie Cole, the mess cleaner, volunteered that a track chart was displayed on the notice board.

He'd barely slung his hammock before he was issued with his flying kit, helmet and survival gear. Numbed by the shock of the Devonport outrage, he was still acting like a zombie. 'You'll be flying in the morning,' they told him before he went below to join 4N8.

He would never forget last night when he had entered the mess for the first time – but what the hell did the incident matter, relative to his agonizing about Gwen's safety? Did it matter a fish's tit whether that bastard Foulgis *was* in the same mess? There were some good blokes too: Rupee Crump had been in the same mess at Culdrose – he was an ex-Merchant Navy man who had rejoined the Navy in 1980. But even Rupee's presence failed to compensate for yesterday's un-pleasant memory, an incident which still left a bad taste, in spite of his anxiety for Gwen.

Seahawk had despatched the *Furious* draft by bus to Penzance, and they were all shipped off by ferry to the carrier in Mount's Bay. As the boat bumped alongside the for'd gangway, he saw for the first time the immensity of this ship. The discharges were spouting through the ship's sides; the flight deck blanked out the sky as he clambered upwards with the others to the top of the gangway. The loud-speakers were braying through the compartments as he trudged for'd along the endless passageways to the regulating office, somewhere on the other side of the ship.

He was still not orientated and it would be weeks before he would be able to find his way about this huge carrier, designed during World War II to survive the hazards which aircraft carriers of that epoch might expect. The result was a warren of over twelve decks of sub-divided compartments, if you counted the island. In this 28,000-ton steel hive toiled nearly a thousand men. In this complex society it was not surprising that the aviators tended to regard themselves as apart from the rest – and vice versa: 'fishheads' or 'deck apes' were seamen; 'WAFUS' (wet and flaming useless) were airmen. Troublemakers could make a feast of the division if they wanted.

After the initial briefing, he had eventually found his way down to 4N8 – down on the fourth deck, tucked away abaft the port lift and the washplaces. He had shoved aside the torn curtain and stepped silently into the mess.

Still in his anorak, he put down his grip and took off his cap. The mess was musty and reeked of stale cigarette smoke. The huddle of men at the far end of the mess looked up from the table at which they were playing cards. One of them, red faced and freckled, climbed to his feet and shoved his neighbour from the settee:

'Osgood?' He stretched out his hand. 'Glad you're in our mess, mate. I heard you were coming.'

'Rupee! I thought I'd never find this place.'

'Got a bunk for you,' Rupee said. 'Up on the port side.'

There was a growl from the end of the table:

'You're flaming lucky, Mister Creep Osgood. Some lesser mortals have to doss down on the deck – like flaming pigs in their own flaming –'

'Rot it, Mick,' one of the others said, the voice feeble.

69

'Give the bugger a chance – he hasn't been 'ere five flaming seconds.'

'That's Toastie Cole,' Rupee said quietly, 'looks after the mess when the duty bod's on watch. He lost his hook, but he still lives here: they're too crowded in the stewards' mess.'

Oz had taken off his anorak and pushed between the bunks where the off-watchmen were sleeping. He held out his hand towards Foulgis:

'I've no hard feelings, Mick,' he said. 'S'pose we forget *Icarus* days?' and he felt the frozen grin on his face as he tried to force a smile.

The dark, pinched face of the Irishman twisted unpleasantly. He looked up, blew a cloud of smoke into Oz' face. Then he crushed out his fag-end.

'Got me hook back,' he said. 'I'm the senior handler in this ship, Osgood. Don't yer forget it.' He looked away, jerked his head towards Toastie. 'Watch out, Toastie. This lot's a flaming creep. He's off to the pigs, if we gets too much up his nostril,' he jeered.

'Lay off it, Foulgis,' Rupee said, grabbing at Oz. 'No need for me to tell you, Oz, what we call him. An 'appy mess, what with Mick the Moaner; and with Toastie kicking up hell because they've cancelled his notice to quit, now there's a war on.'

'Lower deck will be cleared in five minutes time,' the loud-speaker announced from the deck head. 'Hands muster in the hangar.'

Osgood jolted from his brooding. He scrambled from his bunk and threw on his number eights. He slicked back his fair hair, stuck the comb in his hip pocket and, jamming on his cap, hurried down the passageway towards the hangar.

After the sombre lighting of the messdeck, the brightly-lit hangar hoisted Osgood into the world of the immediate. Four Sea Harriers stood at one end and five Sea Kings were lined down the starboard side of the hangar, all in various degrees of servicing – 829 was having one of its Gnome engines replaced. They resembled stranded water-beetles, down here in the hangar, with their blades folded back. The tang of paraffin fuel pervaded the place. On the balcony overhead, running down

70

the port side, he could see the fire watchkeeper who was always on duty. At his command, the two fire curtains could come swinging down at each end, to divide the hangar into sections.

'Close up towards the after end,' the fleet chief master-at-arms shouted, 'Get a hustle on, you lot.'

They fell in, as far as possible by divisions, but in the restricted space order was difficult: Osgood, being one of the last into the hangar, found himself near the front.

'Properly at ease!' the master-at-arms barked.

The officers were assembling at the for'd inboard corner when the commander, John Beclairs, called the company to attention. Osgood saw the figure of Captain Trevellion swinging in through the screen door by the engineering offices and workshops. A packing case had been set in the middle and Trevellion climbed on to it.

'Gather round.'

Osgood felt the pressure behind him; he found himself standing in the front row, barely ten feet from the captain. Trevellion was looking much the same as when he had commanded *Icarus*, but there was something indefinable that had altered him since the loss of his frigate. The crows' feet were deeper at the corners of his eyes, but Trevellion now possessed a steely determination about him which had not been there before. He towered above Bellairs, a squat, thick-set man, standing at ease behind the captain.

'Stand them at ease, Commander.'

Trevellion had no need to raise his voice. In the silence, Osgood heard the wind battering outside and the whirr from the exhaust fans somewhere behind him. He caught sight of a group of squadron engineers caught trying to extricate torpedoes from the magazines. They had halted to control their trollies, up at the for'd end of the hangar.

'It's difficult,' Trevellion began, 'to talk to all of you now that we're at sea, but I've asked the commander to relay what I've got to say to those on watch throughout the ship. I'm sorry I can't meet you all personally, but we are under conditions which none of us have ever experienced before. We've been caretaking for over three decades since the North Atlantic Treaty was signed – and now our stewardship is about to be

71

tested.' He looked around again at the sea of faces and fleetingly caught Osgood's eye.

'I spoke to you when I first took over the ship, at the start of our operational readiness inspection, but I want the new men who have joined, both the normal service entries and the new hostilities-only ratings, to get straight on to the same wave length. The devastation caused by the attack on Guz is something to be shared by all of us.

'I'll define our purpose first,' he said. 'I believe we can't build up a team spirit unless we all know what is our object and for what standards we must aim and work. After twenty-seven years in the Royal Navy, I have come to the belief that there are three supreme things that matter.' He paused: Old Chough certainly had the lads' attention. 'First, belief in our religion – even if some of us have no God, war has a strange habit of changing our attitudes. Second,' Trevellion continued, 'belief in our country and in the freedoms for which we are about to fight; third, belief in, and respect for, each other. The Navy is woefully short of everything – but through holding on to our beliefs, by hard work and by unselfishness, we'll see this battle through.'

Then he was detailing the ship's task for the days ahead:

'Our Force Q has to cover the Canadian convoy on its passage to Oslo. We'll be a hundred miles to the north-west of it at 0500 tomorrow morning – twelve hours time. I'll be altering course to the north-west at 2000 – but I'll have more to say about the coming battle in a moment.

'The first and over-riding essential,' Trevellion went on, 'is discipline – the organized working together of the whole ship for the common good. The old-timers will know just how much organization can make or mar a ship's happiness. Instant obedience of orders is, of course, the first essential and I'll say more of this too in a moment.

'Our ship must be kept spotlessly clean. I hope that being operational will not be made an excuse for allowing this standard to fall. Our health and our ability to fight depends greatly on this...'

The ship was altering to her zigzag and Osgood saw the ranks swaying to her heel, like grass bending to a breeze.

72

Behind the leading ranks he could see the four Sea Harriers, *Furious'* latest addition to her armament. The fifth was on deck, ready to jump after any intruder.

'We're lucky to have inherited a ship's chapel and I hope that as many of you as possible will attend the services. It can, and ought to be, the focus of our inspiration; it can help us together as a team and it does bring us closer to our families.

'I place training very high on my list of priorities. Whether we – and perhaps thousands of others – sink or swim depends on how we acquit ourselves, both in the air with our Sea Kings and Sea Harriers, and in the ship with our EW, sonar and Sea Cats. In war,' he said quietly, 'one man failing to do his duty properly and conscientiously can cause the loss of our ship.'

As if to reinforce the reality of the new existence into which they had all been catapulted, he announced that the Force had last night passed between a double ring of Soviet fleet submarines.

'We know we've sunk two,' he said. 'The second almost committed suicide. I'm sorry that the squadron has suffered its first loss: Sea King 827 is a write-off after ditching while directing a vectac on to the Charlie. I'm glad to welcome her crew back after they were picked up by *Brazen.*' He smiled briefly and added: 'You'll be relieved to know that Aircrewman Gooch – known to most of you as Wally – will be all right and that his back may *not* be permanently damaged. The surgeon commander is taking care of him until we can fly him home.

'Don't forget,' Trevellion went on, 'the correct procedure for stating complaints. If any man feels that he has received an unjust or unfair order, the custom of our service is quite clear: you *must* carry out the order first – then state your complaint afterwards.' He was looking at his watch, anxious, Osgood thought, to return to the bridge.

'In the same way, if any man has any private troubles connected with his home affairs, he can have access to me at any time.' Osgood remembered the help which Trevellion had given him in *Icarus* after Merle had quit. And now Gwen? 'The chaplain's always available at all times to see anyone,' Trevellion continued. 'I think he's been longer in the ship than most of you.' Osgood picked him out, standing relaxed between the officers and the first line of seamen, a large man, with close-cropped, fuzzy hair; everybody called him Matthew, troops and officers alike.

'I'll always do my best to keep you up to date with what's going on – things'll be moving fast during the next week, I expect. I'll let you know immediately what's happening at home, because I know what it's like being without news. I've doubled up on the daily sitrep broadcasts by the first lieutenant – and if mails mean as much to you as they do to me, I'll see to it that we pick up as much as we can – but I think our best plan is to put that side of things behind us for a bit.

'We'll have our work cut out to fight this convoy through to Oslo, sailing north-about around the British Isles. The Soviet Northern Fleet is poised north of Iceland. There are bound to be attacks from their submarines, if these last twelve hours are anything to go by. At 0500 this morning the first all-out Soviet submarine attack took place on HX-OS 1 a few hours after it altered to the north-east after clearing Newfoundland. It's difficult to know the casualties yet, because of radio policy, but two Yank submarines dealt with at least one of the enemy. The tactical control by the US was apparently a great success helping our ASW forces. The convoy is maintaining its speed.'

The frightfulness of what lay ahead was suddenly coming home to the men, but Old Chough had not finished yet.

'Whatever happens to us during the busy days ahead, I want there to be complete understanding between all of you and me, just as I want understanding between officers, petty officers and men – in a spirit of mutual trust and respect. We can do without the time-wasting of the defaulter's table. If I can't get down for my requestmen, then I'm sure the commander will be able to help you.'

Osgood felt uplifted for a moment. There were two objects now for all of them: to fight this convoy through – and survive. If there was any weakening in resolution, none of them were likely to see their homes again.

The captain was standing, his arms by his sides. His grizzled hair showed beneath the sides of his cap. 'Well, that's all,' he said. 'We've got a job to do. Remember the last *Furious* who fought it out during the last war. Many a fine man died to uphold *Furious'* traditions.' He turned, glanced at the commander and stepped down from the crate.

When Osgood reached the Burma Road, he walked aft, towards his mess. In the regulating flat he saw Lieutenant Gamble.

'I wanted to have a word with you,' Hob said, a grim smile on his face, 'but I've been a bit out of routine today.'

'Wally Gooch will be all right then, sir?'

'They'll ground him until we can get him back to Haslar. The spinal column is a sensitive bit of kit.' He jerked his head towards the bulkhead door. 'Come down to my cabin. My oppo is on sortie, so we can talk.'

Osgood's awkwardness soon evaporated in the tin box that was one of the squadron officers' cabins. Gamble sat on the bunk and gave Osgood the chair.

'Wally's out of business for the rest of this trip,' Gamble said directly. 'I've fixed it with the powers that you can replace him to become one of our team. Lieutenant Davies is our observer; Sub-Lieutenant Peterson, the co-pilot. I'm the captain of the aircraft and would like to have you as our aircrewman. The others agree. How about it, Osgood?'

Osgood hesitated, knowing that Gamble was a top-line pilot.

'I'm a sprog at the game yet, sir.' He was watching the pilot carefully, to see whether Hob's interest was merely a charitable gesture: if so, Osgood wanted no part of it. Hob's blue-green eyes were watching him from under those dark and bushy eyebrows which, beneath the straw-coloured hair of his head, gave him such a grotesque appearance. His forehead was freckled, as were the ridges of his cheekbones, and his hair stood up like stubble.

'We'll soon turn you into a hoary old man,' Hob chuckled. 'Anyway, if you prove to be useless, it'll have been my fault. I told you to transfer to the only branch worth being in.'

Osgood smiled. Gamble offered him a cigarette.

Osgood shook his head. 'I've given it up.'

'Got over your problems?' the pilot asked kindly, with no hint of inquisitiveness about the failure of Osgood's marriage.

'Pretty well, sir. But I'm worried at the moment.' Hob listened to his story and, when the silence came, he said quietly:

'My wife's in touch with Mrs Trevellion, who is running the *Icarus* Dependants' Fund. They are trying to help the widows and children. I'll get through to her as soon as we're allowed to break silence. They'll go into Plymouth themselves to see whether they can trace Mrs Fane.'

Osgood nodded and then Gamble asked gently: 'Why don't you see the captain yourself? I can arrange something, if you like.'

Osgood hesitated, backing off. 'He's got a lot on his plate at the moment, sir. I'd rather think about it.'

'Okay, but what about joining us as aircrewman?'

'I'd like to, sir. Thanks.'

'First sortie, tomorrow forenoon.'

'You're flying again – so soon?'

'Yeah – I've a sortie during the middle too: we've no choice in this regiment.' Hob's face was set and a nerve twitched in his left cheek. 'There'll be an inquiry on the loss of my aircraft. There may be a court-martial.'

Osgood remained silent: he was not used yet to the professionalism of the Fleet Air Arm. The buzz was already going round the messdecks that 827 had omitted to ditch the pyrotechnics...

'So long, Osgood,' Hob said, rising from the bunk. 'See you tomorrow morning.'

Osgood went for'd, past the washplaces and the boiler-room bulkheads until he was on the Burma Road again and able to find his way down two decks to 4N8.

Toastie Cole was the only inmate. He looked up antagonistically.

'Where are the others, Toastie?'

'Gone to supper. Mick's got the last dog on the flight deck. Full of himself, he is. Thinks he's the only bleeding handler who can do the job proper.'

'What the hell's up, Toastie?' Oz asked, as he slid on to the bench opposite the unhappy steward.

'I hate Mick's flaming guts.' He spoke softly, his eyes darting towards the bunks which were now all empty.

'Why?'

Toastie wasn't to be drawn. Instead he swigged again at his

beer can. Five empties were lined up in front of him. He twisted a glance at Osgood, his ferrety eyes blurring. He gulped the remainder of the can and his Adam's apple wobbled in his scrawny neck. He then began to weep, his head crooked on his arms. The poor sod was shaking like a blancmange.

'C'mon, Toastie,' Osgood said, clapping Toastie on the shoulder, 'it's not as bad as all that.'

The head jerked up:

'What the flamin' 'ell d'you know about it, then? Mick said you was a flamin' creep.'

'I'm only trying to help, Toastie. There's nobody in the mess. I'm on your side, mate, but I can't help much if you won't tell me what's eating you.'

Toastie rubbed his forearm against his red-rimmed eyes. His sobbing eased and then, staring into the corner of the mess, the words tumbled from him:

'Every word's true, honest, Osgood. You see Mavis, my wife...' The wretched Toastie looked straight at Osgood and then, taking courage again, he spilled his misery. 'She's a whore, a greedy, dirty little bitch – but I love her, Oz, honest I do.' He slashed back his tears with the back of his hand. 'She's a calculating bitch with other men, Oz. Knew it when we married. At first she gave it me hot and strong, mate, but it didn't last. Being a Guz ship, we gets to know each other ashore, those of us who lives in Guz, that is. And one day, that bastard Kotta – *Petty Officer* Kotta,' he sneered, 'came into the pub. It wasn't long before she was after him,' Toastie said savagely. 'I could feel it happening. You know how it is? The little things, bits what don't add up. Then I rumbled that Kotta was always on opposite leave to me. And when I'd get home, she was different, cold and disinterested. I wasn't good enough for her no more. Laughed in my bloody face, told me I was no bloody good in bed – me!' The man would have been laughable had he not be so pathetic. 'And then I had it out man-to-man, like, with Kotta. Told him straight, I did. The bastard laughed – said I should be grateful for his learning her for me. He said if I was a sensible chap, he'd put in a good word for my discharge on compassionate grounds. I slapped in my notice a year ago, before this lot blew up. I want to see Mavis: she'd be different if

I was at home giving her a normal life. But they've slapped down on everything now.'

'Why didn't you see someone?' Osgood asked.

'Scared of Kotta,' Toastie said. 'He's warned me off and he's a big bastard. And Mavis said she'd scarper if I squealed. 'Course, I'm still getting my bit when she can't find no one else.' He sniffed and stabbed at the table-top with his dirty finger tips.

'Then Foulgis joined this flamin' 'ooker.' Cole's laugh was bitter. 'At first, he was right on net with Petty Officer Kotta. I 'spose Kotta must have opened his big mouth and told Foulgis of his affair with a certain lady. I was laughing myself stoopid when Foulgis nicked her from Kotta. She was sampling 'em both at one stage. I found this out after I'd seen Foulgis going ashore with Kotta.'

'Why don't you bugger off, Toastie,' Osgood said quietly. 'She's not worth it, is she?'

''Cos I still loves 'er, Christ, can't you understand that?' He looked up desperately into Osgood's face. 'I'll do anything, any flamin' thing to get myself out of the Navy,' he shouted. 'Any flamin' thing. I've got to get home, Oz,' he shouted wildly. His crazy eyes were fixed across Osgood's shoulder. 'Oh, Christ,' he whispered as his head slumped on the table. Osgood sensed someone had entered the mess behind him. Turning, he saw the brutish figure standing in the gloom by the doorway:

'Didn't you hear the pipe, then?' Petty Officer Kotta was shouting. 'For Exercise, Abandon Ship. Come on, you lot! At the rush – to your stations.' He advanced threateningly and Toastie slunk from the mess like a thrashed whippet.

11

HMS Furious, 14/15 April. Hob Gamble had had enough: half an hour in the wind at his abandon ship station, while the quarter-deck lieutenant-commander waited for his divisional chief to check the muster and to explain the drill to the new boys, had left him hungry and yearning for his bunk. It had been a long, frustrating day and he needed sleep if he was to be fit to fly at dawn the next morning. When they dismissed he went straight down to the wardroom.

The bar was unusually quiet tonight – and not only because they were at war. Those who were enjoying a beer were split into groups, the airmen separated from the ship's officers.

'Beer, Hob?'

'Thanks.' Dunker Davies signed the chit and together they moved over to the group by the pillar. They made way for him and it was obvious what they were discussing.

'Lay off it,' Hob said. 'You know what the man said.'

'You'd think they'd ease up a bit now that we're at war,' someone said. 'Like Churchill did in the last one.'

'What d'you mean?' Grog Peterson asked.

'He told the Admiralty to use their discretion a bit more on court-martials. Chaps were often worn out through no fault of their own.'

'Can't see that happening with our Wings,' someone said. 'It's a pity Duggie has to support him.'

'These cabs cost a lost of money,' someone said.

'So does a pilot,' Hob said and left them. He needed to get his head down. He was still resentful at the way he had been confronted by Craddock, with no suggestion that Hob should ease up for a spell. He wasn't sick, was he? Gamble would carry on flying his next sortie as usual – and, when he was off-duty, he could prepare his written report on the loss of 827. Craddock knew as well as anyone that those six hours off duty were essential for rest. The six hours boiled down to four – an hour debriefing after landing and another kitting up and briefing before taking-off again. Aircrews were flying round the clock now screening Mother.

Hob turned in, thankful to be on his own, for his cabin mate was flying. For the first time since joining the ship, Hob put on his pyjamas. He wanted sleep if he was going to be able to keep up this pace. When the action hotted up, no doubt he would turn in in his clothes and Mae West. Tonight, until he was shaken at 0200, he would remain civilized. He turned on his side, away from the red lightning from the flat outside.

The interview with Wings, Little F and the co had been formal and unpleasant. Craddock had blamed 827's loss squarely on Hob's negligence; not a word about 827 being instrumental in sinking the ssn, perhaps in saving *Oileus* and *Brazen*; nothing about the torpedoes exploding beneath the cab. There was nothing Little F or the co could do. Hob swore silently. He was losing his cool: no better way of ensuring that he would be sub-standard for his next sortie in a few hours time. The worst result of Craddock's decision was the resolute reaction from the aircrewmen.

All the older men, after they had seen Wally Gooch in sick bay, had trooped along to see the fleet chief aircrewman to represent their distaste for the manner in which 827's crew was being treated. Ostensibly, their complaint was that Gooch had been seriously injured in some mysterious way and that the pyrotechnics must be unstable – an argument which obviously could not stand up. Evidently they were trying to show that their loyalty belonged to their pilots and observers. There was a deep feeling of comradeship in the squadron, but this incident was becoming serious.

The aircrewmen were hinting that they might refuse to fly, a threat eagerly fanned in the messes by types like Foulgis, of whose existence the fleet chief was well aware. It was making things awkward for Hob who, unwittingly, had become the victim for their misguided support. To prevent the protest from going further, Hob had sent for Osgood and asked him to make up the crew for the 0300 sortie. The sturdy Devonian said he was ready to fly.

Hob felt bloody-minded tonight. Was this what war was like? Must cold, impersonal professionalism be the only formula by which a modern, complex military arm could operate? The courage, the character of the man himself seemed to have less and less bearing upon the ultimate issue these days. He had often discussed this development with Allie; in the early days, they had agreed that this was why he enjoyed serving in the Fleet Air Arm, where the man counted more than in other branches, save perhaps for the submariners . . . What would she be doing now? It was almost 2200 out here in the Atlantic, so it would be midnight in Wendron where she would be asleep in their bedroom overlooking the patchwork of the Wendron moors. He tried to recall her face but, as always, found her ephemeral image difficult to visualize.

Events were escalating even now: the RAF and Norwegian fighter-bombers' raid had proved abortive in spite of the gallantry with which the attacks were pressed home. Yesterday a Tomahawk attack on Polyarnyy was carried out by one of the latest of the Los Angeles class SSNs but the HE heads were useless against the reinforced pens. The Kremlin had warned that if nuclear warheads were used against their naval bases, the Soviet would retaliate in kind. To emphasize their point, HE missiles were plummeting within the hour upon Newport News and Norfolk. The missiles could have originated only from Echo II SSNs, firing Shaddocks from the US seaboard. This instant retaliation seemed to have halted escalation temporarily, but the many civilian casualties were provoking a howl for revenge. . . .

During these past few hours, disturbing reports had been coming in via the satellite which was now above the horizon: apparently, convoy PH–LH 4 was steaming head-on into a phalanx of submarine attacks from both torpedoes and missiles. The ships were carrying the first reinforcements for Europe; this Le Havre convoy was critical, bringing ammunition, tank and troop reinforcements. Hob had come away from the ops room worried and depressed. How could these determined Soviet submarine attacks fail, with so many targets at which to loose their missiles?

Hob turned on his side and faced the bulkhead. Exhaustion numbed his thoughts until sleep overcame him.

* * * * *

Hob remembered, afterwards, the shuffle of footsteps outside his door, felt the thudding of feet on the deckhead above him. He remembered, too, trying to distinguish the time on the luminous dial of his watch; another hour before they were to shake him at 0200. He must have dropped off again, because it was 0120 before the unaccustomed silence woke him from his sleep – like home after a spell at sea, when he couldn't sleep for the first night because of the silence. Now, all he could hear was the huffing of the ventilation. He rolled from his bunk, flung on his clothes and hurried up the ladders towards the bridge; he would make for the starboard wing on the opposite side from Flyco, to discover what was going on: if the ship was at action stations he would have heard the bugle or the rattlers. He shoved against the screen door and stepped out on to the wing, in the lee from the wind. It was cold; he should have worn his sweater. He raised his hand to shield his eyes from the bright-ness of the searchlight projector being trained behind him by a signalman. Hob could hear the hissing of the arcs and the blue-white beam was blinding as it swept across the sea down the starboard side.

'What's up?' Hob asked the starboard lookout who was sweeping the horizon through binoculars. An oblong ellipse appeared on the surface of the sea where the white horses were curling lazily.

The lookout lowered his glasses and Hob saw the surprise in the man's eyes:

'Man overboard, sir', he said. 'It's been twenty minutes now.'

He jammed the eyepieces back into his eyes as an armed landing craft butted into the ellipse of blue light. Hob saw the calcium flares spluttering in the cold, green sea where they streamed from the empty lifebuoy. Then a second ALC forged into sight, its ramp fringed by Royal Marines searching for the missing man. Someone was out there fighting for his life, able to see the ship as he yelled to attract attention . . . and then Hob heard the loud-speaker blaring behind him from the screen:

'Lieutenant Gamble, Lieutenant Gamble – 394.'

Hob's stomach dropped. He swung open the screen door and darted into the met. office where he could dial the number.

'Lieutenant Gamble here.'

'Master-at-arms, sir. You should be in the wardroom for the muster.'

Hob caught the reproach in the jaunty's voice. He clattered down the ladders to the wardroom, where he expected a jocular reception but, as he rushed along the passageway, the door burst open. The first of the officers were streaming back to their cabins.

'What's up?' Hob asked the petty officer steward who was emerging from the pantry.

'No one adrift, sir,' he said. 'That hoaxer again.'

'Happened before?'

'Yes, sir. Third time this commission. Someone'll get killed. Excuse me, sir,' and he hurried for'd towards his mess.

Hob waited for the crush to subside before entering the ante-room. It was 0150, so it would be pointless to turn in again before the 0230 briefing. He slumped on to the settee and stared around the empty ante-room. He would grab himself a cup of cocoa from the crew's mess-room. He was about to leave when the loud-speaker snicked on above him:

'D'ye hear there? This is the captain speaking...'

Hob sat up, reached for his cap.

'We are now hoisting the two ALCS. For this evolution you all know that the ship must be stopped, just as I was forced to take off her way while we lowered these large craft safely. The evolution is always dangerous at night. The lifebuoy sentry has carried out his duty; he can't ignore a "man overboard" passed over the telephone.' The captain paused and Hob could hear the officer of the watch talking quietly in the background.

'We are now at war and I cannot risk the safety of this ship again by stopping to search for a man who falls overboard. A stopped ship is a sitting duck to a submarine. The squadron is too stretched to provide emergency cover, so I regret that any man falling overboard will most certainly lose his life at night. I repeat, I cannot risk again disclosing our position by burning signal projectors or sending away the boats.

'Someone is being deliberately subversive in this ship. He

must be found and brought before me.' He ended briskly: 'Now let's get on with the war.'

Hob left the wardroom and climbed up to the crew's mess-room. He was stirring his cocoa when the duty steward turned to him, the telephone held in his hand:

'For the senior pilot, sir. You're wanted in Flyco.'

It was very dark and very quiet in the small flat outside the mini-bridge from which flying operations were conducted. Hob halted for a moment to collect himself and to square off his rig: he was beginning to suffer the same feeling of insecurity as when he had once been a sprog member of the squadron. He peered through the glass window and watched the activity down on the flight deck where the marshals were bringing in a couple of helos from the inner screen. The glow from the marshals' fluorescent bats danced like fireflies, while the phosphorescence from the tail rotors spun in spectral circles. The night-lighting bathed the whole scene in an eerie sheen, invisible from sea-ward but providing enough light in which to operate flying stations. There were the fire parties in their fearnought suits, moon men, standing by with their trolleys of foam – and over-whelming all, the whine and scream of the jets which was part of their lives...

'That you, Gamble?'

'Yes, sir.'

On Craddock's right, Hob could distinguish the smaller figure of Little F crouched in his seat as he supervised the flight deck below him, his communication number at another desk on his right. Duggie Mann, the co, was in Flyco too, leaning against the for'd window.

There was no mistaking the tone of Wing's question: wags said he'd acquired that nutmeg-grater voice from trying to talk to his observer in the rear seat of a Stringbag.

'What's this about the aircrewmen, Gamble?' he rasped. 'The fleet chief's been up to see me.' The anger in Craddock's voice was evident enough, but Hob felt the resentment rising also within himself.

'They're not happy about yesterday's incident, sir. The grapevine's fairly accurate, I'd say.'

84

'Okay. Explain. You're the senior pilot.'

'They think it's unsafe to fly, sir, until the pyrotechnics have been checked in all the aircraft. And, sir . . .'

'Yes?'

'They think it unfair to threaten us – me – sir, with a court-martial for the loss of 827 yesterday.' Hob swallowed in the dim lighting. The interminable silence was worse than the expected explosion, but he did not give a damn now. He waited, tense, while behind him, the communication rating carried on unconcernedly with his procedures.

'I see. And what do they propose to do about all this?' Wings asked, his voice low and very controlled.

'They don't want to fly, sir.' Hob stood his ground, then added quietly, 'I can't help it, sir, if they feel your decision's unjust.'

Little F turned in his seat. He was a good sort, but his reaction could have been no other:

'You're the senior pilot, Gamble. You ought to be able to squash this sort of thing.'

'I've tried to, sir. But it's all happened pretty swiftly. I've only just heard about it myself. It's their way of expressing loyalty to their crews, I think – nothing more . . .'

'Funny way of doing it.' The sonorous tones of the Squadron co were audible for the first time. 'It's a technical mutiny, Lieutenant Gamble.'

Hob hesitated, choosing his words carefully. He was aware that the bridge personnel behind him were very quiet, eavesdropping on the proceedings in Flyco.

'No, sir. I don't agree.' He turned back to Craddock. 'With respect, sir, it's only a complaint as yet.'

Craddock stood motionless. Hob faced him squarely, watching the towering figure etched against the indigo of the windows. In the silence, he could hear one of the cabs outside screaming to full power as it prepared to lift off.

'Ready for your sortie, Gamble?' Craddock asked abruptly.

'Yes, sir,' Hob replied, surprised. He declined to add that his back still ached like hell.

'Crew complete?'

'Yes, sir.'

'Who's your aircrewman?'

'Aircrewman Osgood, sir. He's just joined and done one sortie. He's okay, sir.'

'Carry on, Gamble,' Wings snapped.

'Aye, aye, sir.' He saluted and turned smartly. He could feel the silence behind him as he quit Flyco. He slid open the screen door and climbed down the ladders to the briefing room.

12

Sea King 833, 15 April. It was 0330 when Hob saw the silver streak of first light touch the underside of the dark cloud layers stretching from horizon to horizon. Up at fifteen hundred feet in Sea King 833, in company with 825, they were at last monitoring their Jez field ninety miles ahead of *Furious.* Mother was doubling back to make her rendezvous position ahead of the convoy; at 0500 she should be well on the up-threat side of the Canadian convoy.

'We'll move to the south-west when we've finished this one,' Dunker called from the back. 'That'll put us right between Mother and the convoy.'

'Okay, Dunker,' Hob replied. 'What's our Charlie-time?'

'0435. That'll give us plenty of time to find Mother.'

They could hear the Canadian commodore already piping up on UHF as he tried to shepherd his flock into station before the dangerous period of twilight. Evidently they had given up electronic silence after the mauling they had received last night, when they turned up to the north-eastward.

Dunker and 825 had been out of touch with Mother for over three-quarters of an hour, so it would be good to chat with the convoy once they had contacted it. Eavesdropping on the convoy's internal frequency was revealing disquieting news: PH–LH 4 had been almost obliterated by a savage missile attack from an estimated force of seventeen Soviet SSNs. Figures were still unreliable, but it seemed that almost the entire convoy had been wiped out, including half the considerable escort.

'Look, Hob,' Grog snapped. 'There it is.'

Hob turned the cab to port, the better to see. Twilight had now merged into a grey dawn and far to the south-west he could make out the smudges of the leading ships.

'Jez completed,' he heard Osgood reporting to Dunker, who then came in, giving the new heading towards the convoy.

They still kept radar silence, but in a few minutes, when within UHF range, they would report to the commodore.

'Impressive, ain't it?' Grog remarked.

Even during the largest of the Nato exercises, Hob had never seen anything like this. The sea was a silver shimmering bowl beneath them, the breaking waves frothing round the bows and wakes of the convoy. As Hob lost height, preparing for the next Jez, he began to pick out the ships in the five columns.

In the van of the centre column was the commodore's ship, his burgee streaming proudly from the halyards abaft the bridge. She looked like the ex-*France*, the swash-buckling ship with elegant lines which the Norwegians had bought and renamed *Norway*. Hob counted four ships astern of her, all modern, some container, some bulk, others general cargo. There must be five miles between each and at least six between the centre column and its neighbours. Probably another five miles separated the outer column from the intermediate, a total width of twenty-two miles: the convoy must cover 330 square miles. The ships were deliberately not following in each others' wakes while they zigzagged. Tail-end Charlie was obviously having trouble keeping up: an escorting frigate was wheeling astern of her charges and screening one ship which, even from up here, seemed to be badly knocked about amidships.

Ungava Bay, one of the most important in the eighteen-ship convoy, was easily recognizable tucked away in the second column, the second ship from the rear. With her huge car decks, the ship was specially designed for awkward loads. The heavy stuff stowed well below: the cranes, tank-transporters and earth-shifting gear. The army tracked vehicles were normally awkward cargo but *Ungava Bay*'s car decks easily coped with the lot. The Canadian Division's small arms ammunition, spares and light guns were stowed in container boxes on deck, almost to the height of the bridge.

'The commodore's just signalled,' reported Dunker. 'He wants to share us with Mother so that the Yanks can go home to cover the BO–EU 2 convoy. I suggest we screen thirty miles ahead until Mother joins.'

'Okay, Dunker. Heading?'

'058°. They want us to act as visual link with Mother.'

'Heading 058°,' Hob confirmed. 'Fifteen hundred feet, hundred knots.'

'Fine. That'll give me time to take down the commodore's signals. He's passing casualty details now.'

Hob and Grog had little to do now but listen to Dunker decoding the sitreps. Hob glanced at Grog when the first one came in: the nuclear onslaught on PH–LH 4 had all but annihilated it, without warning. Among the twenty-eight ships overwhelmed had been nine Frenchmen. A message had just come in from ACLANT indicating that France had declared herself this morning for the Western Allies. Her *force de frappe* of five second-generation SSBNS was at the disposal of Nato, as was her fleet. ACLANT was immediately deploying French surface units into the Atlantic to relieve STANAVFORLANT, whose mission was to fill the void left by the Carrier Striking Force being forced to dash down south to the Azores. All French land forces were mobilized and were taking up their positions on the central plain beside their Nato friends.

Just as disconcerting for Hob and the rest of the crew was the report that five choppers had been brought down when attacking lone, detached SSNS. So far, no cause could be given, but it was assumed that enemy submarines possessed an unknown capability for destroying hovering helicopters. Grog made a wry face as he glanced at Hob. 'Seems to bear out your *Icarus* skylark, Hob,' he volunteered cheerfully. MOD was still reticent, but a code name, Anvil, had been allocated to the suspected retaliatory weapon.

The next item was unexpected. In accordance with a previous Allied warning to the Soviets, Nato ships were now to use, when suitable, nuclear depth bombs (NDBS) against confirmed enemy sub. contacts. Each sortie of 814 Squadron's ASW Sea Kings was to be armed with at least one NDB.

'Phew!' Hob muttered. 'Hotting up a bit.'

The commodore then passed his convoy disposition, emphasizing that *Valiant*, one of the oldest fleet submarines, was acting independently twenty miles ahead of the convoy.

'That's all,' Dunker reported. 'Stand by to lay, Ozzie.'

Then, as Hob eased to ninety knots, he heard the observer recording a Flash Report from ACLANT.

'*Flash – flash – flash!*' Hob heard Dunker repeating. 'Major enemy surface units steering south-east from Cape Farewell.' Then another report, probably as a result of the Nimrod and the sosus analyses:

'Nine ssns confirmed on a nw–se line crossing hx track, centre of axis 35°W.'

'That'll be enough to keep Force Q awake,' Dunker added. 'Hold your heading at that, Hob. *Drop, drop, drop.*'

Hob watched the sonobuoys tipping into the sea. Neither he nor Grog had much to say: ahead, an enemy strking force, taking advantage of the changing dispositions in the Nato forces, had slipped through the Greenland–Iceland gap. Major units of the Northern Fleet were charging southward to challenge Force Q and the Canadian convoy it was shielding.

'Let's hope the Harriers are airborne,' Grog said.

'Druce won't miss a trick,' Hob said. 'I can imagine his nostrils breathing fire and brimstone already.'

'That's what I'm afraid of,' Grog said quietly. 'He's too bloody brave.'

But in both pilots' minds lurked an ugly thought. At least nine enemy ssns lay in wait, less than 250 miles ahead. It was the squadron's job to winkle them out and to destroy them, with ndbs if need be. No one liked using these depth-bombs; but neither did the Sea King crews relish being shot from the sky by the mysterious Anvil.

'Field laid,' Dunker reported. 'Heading 350°.'

The drill continued, but in the shuddering, roaring machine each man was marooned by his own thoughts.

13

HMS Furious, 15/16 April. Sea Kings 833 and 829 landed at 0520 on spots 5 and 3. The handlers took longer than usual as they struggled in the wind to secure the lashings.

Aircrewman Osgood slid open the door and jumped on to the deck. Crouching against the gale, they leaned to the great ship's motion as she pitched and yawed in the quartering sea. Her massive bow rose majestically as she lifted to the swell racing beneath her forefoot; the flight deck canted, the ship rolling rhythmically like the dignified matron she was. The screen door slammed shut behind them. Hob signed off the aircraft and then they made their way down into the warmth 'tween decks. A rapid debriefing, coffee and something to eat and Osgood would crash out in record time: he was pooped.

But the debriefing was not the crisp routine to which they were accustomed. The ops officer was determined to bring them up to date on the tactical situation in the Atlantic. Osgood was content, as he loosened his overalls and lolled back on the benches; the fug and the sudden lifting of tension after four hours of concentration in Sea King 833 were a sensual pleasure. The voice of the ops officer droned on. The bright glare of the Atlantic map which showed on the screen was all that prevented him from nodding off . . . but the precarious situation of Force Q and the Canadian convoy for the next thirty-six hours made him sit up.

Three red lines were slashed across the convoy's trackline: A, the nearest within a day's steaming; B, the central, close to Rockall which Force Q should reach before midnight on Wednesday; and C, the furthest, clipping the edge of the Faeroes Bank, where the convoy had to turn to starboard at Position Juliett, for the passage through the Orkneys–Shetland gap. The enemy submarine lines were crescent-shaped, curving to contain the advance of the convoys. The Nimrods, virtually defenceless from Soviet long-range aircraft, had whittled down the SOSUS detections and a clear picture had emerged: line A consisted of thirty-plus SSNs; B, twenty; and C, four. All SSNs were some hundred miles apart. As the convoy approached line A, the offensive patrol line was closing, like the claws of a crab. At a speed of thirty knots, two attacking submarines could straddle the HX convoy within ninety minutes – a minimum of six SSNs could concentrate on the convoy, if necessary. *Valiant*, the British SSN patrolling independently ahead of the convoy, would have a field day, once she got in among them. The enemy could also stand off at horizon range to attack with sub-surface missiles, if he wanted.

'So there you are, gentlemen,' the ops officer said. 'That's our war for the next few days, providing what's going on north of us doesn't upset the pigeon loft. The surface situation is developing rapidly and changing minute by minute.' His pointer tipped the red and blue crosses confronting each other 420 miles due north of *Furious*' present position – three hundred miles east of Greenland's Cape Farewell.

'The Soviet High Command,' he continued, 'seems to have decided to risk all on one throw. They're poised for an out-and-out victory in the Atlantic, playing one colossal gamble. They seem to have rejected the cautious strategy of a reserve second strike. They're trying to cut our Atlantic lifeline at one fell swoop.

'Look at the present disposition of its strike group – *Kiev* among them.' His pointer tapped the screen again east of Cape Farewell. 'If our Carrier Striking Force was not between us and the enemy, he could wipe out HX–OS tonight.' He glanced at them all, then continued:

'The two fleets are playing cat-and-mouse at the moment: our Carrier Striking Force refuses to be drawn. It's keeping open its options in case the enemy's striking group decides to leave us alone and attacks instead the BO–EU and NY–AN convoys which will be within range tomorrow. Our Carrier Striking Force is ready for anything the enemy chooses to chuck at it: the Soviets are unlikely to turn south-west, because that would foul up their submarine lines. You can see, gentlemen, how awkward it is for us to be losing Striking Group One at this moment, though our Carrier Striking Force, as soon as it is convinced that the convoys are safe, will then move south-east to replace Carrier Striking Group One. STANAFORLANT is steaming westwards to fill the vacuum astern of us, while the convoys from America move across.'

To Osgood, trying to keep awake, the possible surface action between the giants seemed too remote, too unreal. All he craved was to get in some zeds before his next sortie.

Though it was not an unseemly rush when they made for the door, little time was wasted in dispersing. For Osgood, 4N8 mess would be a haven at this moment, after a bit of breakfast.

For the helicopter crews, their first experience of war at sea was one of gruelling work and boredom: sortie, food, sleep, sortie. The routine became automatic. After four hours of Jez runs ahead of the carrier, Osgood and the others in 833 were becoming used to the pear-shaped NDB slung beneath the cab. *Furious*, though 110 miles on the up-threat side of the convoy, was zigzagging ninety miles astern of her far-flung ASW screen with 833 forming the spear-head. After four hours, Osgood felt the tension caused by apprehension of imminent action beginning to lessen ... but when, for the second time that day, he scuttled across the flight deck, he was longing for his bunk. The second debriefing finished promptly at 1900; he swallowed a quick supper and hurried down to 4N8.

The atmosphere in the mess was blue with smoke. Heads stuck out from between the curtains of the bunks as the occupants chi-akked among themselves and watched a game of cards at the table below where Rupee and a leading radio operator were challenging Foulgis and another handler. As Osgood quietly stripped to his underclothes and swung himself up to his pit, he sensed for the first time a feeling of friendliness in the cramped quarters. He lay back, arms crossed behind his head, watching, feeling good after the hot food. Allowing drowsiness to creep over him, he fished his wallet from under his pillow and surreptitiously extracted the colour snap of Gwen.

Hob Gamble had spoken to him again: they would be seeing the captain once the pressure of this convoy operation eased. The request had got past the commander and now it was only a matter of waiting. As soon as radio silence was lifted, the

Plymouth Welfare people would be investigating also. Osgood thrust Gwen's photo back into his wallet as he heard raised voices round the table: Foulgis, for sure, was accusing Rupee of cheating. Tempers were flaring, the card players becoming angrily strident.

'Cut it out,' another watchkeeper yelled from a lower bunk. 'Stop that bloody noise.'

Osgood flipped back his curtain. Rupee was gathering up the cards. 'Give the watchkeepers a chance to sleep,' another man said.

Foulgis looked up and saw Osgood watching from the upper bunk.

'What you gawping at, Osgood?' Foulgis snarled. 'Disturbing your dreams, am I?' He moved beneath the bunk, a smirk on his face as he turned back towards the others:

'We had a fire in *Icarus*, Rupee,' he went on. 'The leading MEM, Niv Fane, was burnt to death. Poor bugger left a wife and two kids.' Foulgis swung round and jabbed a finger towards Osgood:

'This creep took Niv's wedding ring round to the widow in Guz.' He laughed coarsely. 'He's been having it off with her ever since,' he leered. 'Wasted no time. Me brother-in-law lives in the next street.'

Something snapped inside Osgood. He swung down from his bunk. He leaped towards Foulgis, grabbing the Irishman's shirt collar, and slammed his fist into the sneering face.

'Grab 'em!' Rupee shouted to the amazed onlookers, as they tried to separate the struggling adversaries. The two men were facing each other, their arms held by their messmates.

'Any more of that, Foulgis,' Osgood panted, trying to regain control of himself, 'and I'll fix you, mate, once and for all.'

'Get stuffed,' the Irishman shouted, as the voice of the divisional PO rasped from the doorway:

'Come on, you noisy lot of bastards,' Kotta called. 'Time you squared off for rounds.'

In the silence Rupee settled the table, while the others made themselves scarce. Foulgis sat down, a forced grin on his face as he gazed up at the petty officer.

'On your feet, Foulgis,' Kotta fumed. 'You heard the order.'

Foulgis flipped the cards, began shuffling for another hand; he peered up, his dark eyes flickering with amused contempt.

'You mustn't speak to me like that, Petty Officer. You ought to be working with me as a team-mate, remember?' Then he rose slowly to his feet. The mess had almost emptied. Osgood, who had regained his bunk, closed the curtains. He'd had enough and craved sleep: he had the 0300 sortie again. He'd have a shower and a bite to eat when they shook him.

Kotta was striding towards the insolent aircraft handler. Through the gap in his curtains, Osgood watched the scene, the hulking PO literally carmine in the face. His ham hands were trembling.

'Lay a hand on me, Petty Officer Kotta, and I'll run you in.' Foulgis' laugh grated. 'We're not kids down here. You forget this is a leading hands' mess, don't you?' he sneered, his piggy eyes glistening with hatred. He turned towards the miserable Cole: 'We can learn him a thing or two, can't we, Toastie?'

Cole whispered something to Kotta, then stood back to allow the two men to shove past him.

'I'll see you outside, Foulgis.' Kotta spat the words. 'C'mon – *move*. At the rush.' He shoved Foulgis hard. The handler half-fell, stumbling from the mess.

No one spoke. As Osgood turned on his side, he heard Rupee laughing nervously outside with the dutymen who were waiting for rounds. Osgood turned over and fell asleep immediately.

'Hey, Osgood,' an aircrewman growled, jabbing at his bunk. 'Five minutes. It's 0205.'

The dutymen got one shake only – no second chance now, so Osgood slipped from his bunk before dropping off again. In the semi-darkness, he fumbled in his locker for his towel and soap, and shuffled quietly from the snoring mess for'd to the wash-places.

At this hour of the morning there would be no queue for the showers; no switching off of a neighbour's hot tap which caused a sudden surge of pressure in one's own shower – sometimes with devastating results – a hazard which had led to the custom of bellowing, 'Switching off,' when turning off a hot tap.

In the dank shower room the shower-heads drooped in rows

like sunflowers. Osgood chose the furthest – the cleanest – and stuffed his towel behind the screen. A cold draught was whipping through the washplace and he tried to shut the half-open door – but the spring was defective and the door swung back. He slammed shut the metal partition of his cubicle and stripped off. The water was scalding hot.

A few minutes later, as he turned off both taps and squeezed the water from his hair, he heard a sneering voice he could identify anywhere.

'I can have a piss, can't I, Kotta, without you hanging around?'

Osgood dried himself slowly, keeping quiet. Kotta seemed to be moving up the passage outside. It was his voice which called in an undertone from the for'd end of the shower room:

'I'm on the same watchkeeping roster as you, Foulgis. You've gone too far: I'm not having your insolence see?' Osgood, motionless behind the steel door, sensed the fury in the PO's voice.

'You're a screwball, Kotta,' Foulgis called. 'Mavis is dead right: you're as useless as a PO as what you are to her.' The handler was shuffling along the tiled deck.

'You coming out? Or do I come in and get you?' Kotta said.

Foulgis laughed. 'Don't be so flaming stupid. These aren't the POs heads. I'll run you in, you sod, if you lay a finger on me.'

Osgood could hear the man's breathing as he slopped in his sandals through the half-open door.

'We'll see about that,' Osgood heard Kotta growl – then the thump of a blow.

'*You bastard.*' Foulgis didn't hide the fear in his voice, as he cowered from the vicious attack. 'You're a flaming bad loser. Can't take it, Kotta?'

Osgood had finished drying himself, but stood motionless while the fight developed outside, both men grunting. They seemed to have stopped for a breather, their words coming between gasps:

'You could have had her, if you'd listened,' Foulgis taunted. 'Told you, but you wouldn't listen.'

'What you driving at?' Kotta gasped, struggling for breath.

'It's not size what counts, you conceited bum.'

Osgood heard someone spit – then another blow and Foulgis was muttering:

'Lay off, Kotta. And stop hounding – me – in this flaming ship – or I'll take you to the chief.'

They were exhausted, panting in the red gloom outside. In his cubicle, Osgood groped for his washing things.

'You wouldn't risk it, with Toastie here.' There was a hint of panic in Kotta's voice. 'Hey – put that away, you Irish bastard . . .'

There was a grunt from Kotta and then they were scrambling for'd. Osgood's soap slithered to the tiled deck and he had to go down on to his knees to retrieve it. By the time he had emerged through the door, the passageway was empty.

He hesitated. What if Foulgis *had* drawn a knife? Osgood flipped back the clip, leaned against the bulkhead door.

The force of the wind from the open space of the side lift brought him up all-standing. It was very dark here, where the bollards were sited for the RAS wires. He could hear the roar and pounding of the seas. It was always cold when the lift doors were open, where the spray flew and the wind lashed. The sombre red of the night-lighting cast an eerie gloom on the lift.

Osgood halted in his tracks. On the far side of the open space beside the lift, a shadowy figure crouched, its legs pumping like pistons. Something tumbled over the edge and vanished into the night. The figure paused for a second, peering over the side into the darkness. Then, as a rat scuttles in the sewers, he was gone, shrouded in the shadows.

Osgood rushed for'd, his heart pumping. The ship's roll made him stumble, sliding across the wet steel deck. Braking himself with his hands, he stopped by the edge. He glimpsed the threshing waves, heard the roaring in the black night. As he regained his balance, he felt a warm stickiness where his hands had supported him on the plating.

He was shivering as he backed away from the dark corner. He thought he heard someone yelling behind him, but he ran on down the passageway. Someone in a blue anorak was just disappearing through the bulkhead door as he grabbed the telephone he found in the first flat he reached. Osgood saw the smeared blood on the receiver. He spun the dial.

'Bridge?' the calm voice, remote, from somewhere in another world, answered calmly.

'Man overboard, port side!' Osgood shouted. 'Man over!'

He slammed the receiver back on its rest, stared at the blood on his crimson hand. He rushed across to the other side, climbed the ladder and ran to the flat which held the regulating office. It was quiet here, silent in the middle watch. As he heard the Man Over bells ringing faintly somewhere aft, he pushed into the cabin where the fleet master-at-arms was already tumbling from his bunk.

'Master!' he shouted, 'Master-at-Arms, a man's been murdered.'

14

HMS Furious, 16 April. Fleet Master-at-Arms David Legge had turned in late on that Tuesday night. Several stupid irritations, some of them originated by senior men who should have known better, had kept him up. His sleep had been fitful, his mind disturbed by reports from the petty officers' mess. Now he heard the discordant, braying alarm bells.

'*Overboard! Man Overboard.*'

As he rolled from his bunk, his curtains swished apart.

'What the –?' he blurted. A man he did not recognize burst inside the cabin, a towel around his middle. His face was grey and blood was smeared across his cheek and chin. His right hand was crimson and wet.

'Murdered? How d'you know?' Legge snapped. 'What's your name?'

'Osgood,' the man gasped. 'Aircrewman. 4n8.'

'Get hold of yourself, son. Here – take my chair.'

The fleet master-at-arms listened impatiently as the leading hand spilled his yarn. 'Okay,' he told him. 'I'll get the duty regulating PO to take it down in writing.' Legge showed him the door. 'Get yourself cleaned up and wait in the regulating office while I deal with the Man Over musters.'

'I'm due for briefing at 0230, sir,' the wild-eyed aircrewman said. He stood trembling with cold and shock, in the draughty flat. 'Sortie's at 0300.'

'Right,' Legge snapped. 'Report to me as soon as you get back.' He watched as the shattered man scurried aft, towards the leading hands' overflow mess, whence earlier worrying reports had originated. The regulating staff were gathering morosely, but all were cynically convinced that the hoaxer was up to his tricks again. Legge took over the broadcast mike himself:

'D'you hear there?' he announced. 'This is the fleet

master-at-arms speaking. Report as soon as your mess musters are checked.'

There was nothing to do but wait. The ship's life went on, and those on duty would be allowed for. While waiting for the reports, Legge would find the Commander, who would be interested to learn of the developments. Legge returned to his cabin, pulled on his trousers and white sweater, squared his cap upon his grizzled head and hurried aft. He nipped up the ladder on to the next deck. At the top, a bulky figure was waiting in the shadows of the big fan.

'Thanks,' Legge said. He was hurrying by when the man called after him:

'Master?'

'Yes? Why aren't you at your muster?' He hardly recognized the twisted face of the petty officer.

'What's up, Petty Officer Kotta?' Legge asked irritably. 'I'm pushed – Man Over muster.'

'I must tell you something,' the dishevelled PO stammered.

Trevellion was also in a state of half-consciousness when he registered through the open doorway of his sea-cabin the yell from the officer of the watch, then the man overboard alarm. His stomach sinking, Trevellion pulled on his reefer; in his slippers and pyjama trousers, he hurried to the bridge.

'Lifebuoys gone, sir,' the young lieutenant reported.

'When's the next zig?'

'Three minutes, sir. Twenty degrees to port.'

Trevellion snatched his binoculars from the back of his captain's chair and nipped out to the starboard wing. The ship was pitching heavily and he had to wedge himself into the corner. Just visible, the calcium flares were spluttering orange flames of smoke on each side of the wake.

He shouted into the bridge, sure that his communications yeoman would be there:

'Yeoman, tell *Phoebe* to search for the missing man. She's not to fall more than five miles astern of us and is to rejoin after ten minutes. Inform the flag lieutenant.'

'Aye, aye, sir.'

As Pasco hurried in from the cold, he heard the projector

clattering, saw the blue signal light flashing across the starboard quarter. Craddock was waiting for him by the entrance to Flyco.

'Couldn't be at a worse moment, sir,' he said. 'Between sorties and I've no stand-by. We're stretched to the limit and arming with NDBs has thrown my roster out of phase.'

'All right, Wings. Carry on with your flying. The Force comes first.' The captain, sickened by the repetition of the hoaxer's lunacy, walked to the for'd window. The night was black outside, the spray sweeping upwards in fine plumes and drenching even the bridge windows. In spite of what Trevellion had told his ship's company, his instincts were to fly off an emergency Sea King for the missing man – more to soothe his own conscience, because search and recovery would be impossible in these conditions.

'Message passed, sir. *Phoebe* is breaking away to search.'

'Thanks, Yeoman.'

'Altering twenty degrees to port, sir,' the officer of the watch was calling. '*Gloucester*, *Brazen*, *Köln*, and *Oileus* conforming.'

'Very good,' Trevellion acknowledged from the for'd window. What was going wrong in his ship? One of the buzzes suggested that the hoaxer was in the overflow mess, 4N8. A disrated steward, Cole, had been acting in a 'demented' way because of family troubles. The commmander was keeping an eye on Cole, and Bellairs was one of the best executive officers Pascoe had yet encountered.

Trevellion wished he enjoyed the same confidence in his prickly Wings. Craddock must be one of the last of the old breed of pilots, but his inflexible methods were causing resentment: of that, Trevellion, always sensitive to atmosphere, was becoming convinced. Throwing the book at Lieutenant Gamble, Trevellion felt sure, had been intended to show that this was war, when humanity had to be left out of the scheme of things for the sake of efficiency. Discipline was a hard task-master sometimes; but, as Craddock had emphasized, war was war and he intended to instil a tough philosophy in his airmen.

'Captain, sir?'

He turned to see Bellairs and Legge, the master-at-arms, standing behind him.

'Not a hoax this time, sir,' Bellairs said.

Trevellion said nothing. So he had allowed a man to drown, for the sake of the Force. '*Phoebe* might still pick him up,' he said.

'Don't think so, sir,' the master said. 'He was dead when he went over the side.' The steady, square-set fleet chief hesitated.

'Come to the chart house,' Trevellion said, leading the way to the after end of the bridge. They sat on the chart house settee, the captain taking the high stool.

'Leading Handler Foulgis, 4N8 mess, sir, missing from muster.'

'How d'you know he was dead?'

'He was murdered, sir,' the master said quietly. 'I've had two different versions – each with a different motive.'

Trevellion listened to what had been discovered. Foulgis and Osgood hated each other's guts apparently, but there were some odd anomalies in the evidence: things pointed towards Osgood but PO Kotta, it seemed, could not be ruled out as a suspect. Each man was accusing the other and there had been no time to interview anyone.

'I've placed them both under open arrest,' Bellairs said, 'until they can see you, sir. They're carrying on with their duties while we investigate.'

Trevellion nodded: the war had to go on.

'John, see to the MOD signal for the next of kin, please. Report on the murder as soon as possible. Ask the chaplain to help them, if they need him.'

Bellairs saluted and the two men left. Trevellion felt a desolation he had experienced rarely in his life: how could men hate so intensely that they could kill their own messmates? Emotion must be running high somewhere and his ship's officers had better get to the bottom of it. The muted defiance of the aircrewmen yesterday was serious: their motives were well-intentioned, but their protests had not gone unnoticed in the messdecks. Trevellion felt an unease which he had experienced once before in his service life, when he had joined *Icarus* at Bermuda. Those problems had soon sorted themselves out – and he hoped that the same common sense would prevail in *Furious*.

The aircrewmen were now carrying out their duties normally, in spite of Craddock's determination to stick to his court-martial decision. The fact that such a fine bunch were kicking up a shindy indicated a serious blunder on the part of his controversial Wings ... and Trevellion turned to stroll to the after end of the bridge.

The quiet efficiency of Flyco seemed undisturbed as Little F supervised the flying operations. The 0300 sortie was becoming airborne, the winking lights flashing, the batsmen's torches wreathing in the violet lighting of the flight deck. 833 was increasing to full power on spot 4, the scream of her engines reaching even to the bridge.

These modern fliers were of similar fibre to their forebears, Trevellion thought. They shared the same denigrating humour, the identical unpretentious professionalism; and they held a similar disregard for danger as did their fathers ... there she went, 833, lifting clear of spot 4, canting on her side, sheering over the carrier's side, parallel for an instant, then forging ahead into the night. The others were following her swiftly, only seconds behind ... an efficient bunch, kept so only by their own efforts. These next few weeks would prove whether these decades of training would stand up to the test of war. Trevellion knew that soon he would be witnessing the first casualties. The battle reports from the Soviet attacks on the escorted convoys farther south were worrying: too many choppers were being lost, probably shot down by the mysterious Anvil.

'The admiral's in the ops room, sir,' the flag lieutenant reported quietly behind him. 'When you've got a minute, sir.'

'Right, flags. I'll be down.' It was 0320 already: less than forty-five minutes before dawn, the hour when the enemy submarines *must* attack, if they intended to interfere with the convoy. It was surprising that they had not yet shown more aggressiveness, because night and low visibility were a decided disadvantage for ASW choppers.

The ops room crew was calmly going about its business, the glow from the displays providing much of the light in the compartment. The HCO was busy, monitoring the 0300 sortie and recovering the helicopters which had done their stint.

'Morning, Pascoe.' Rear-Admiral Roderick Druce was as fresh as an Olympic runner waiting for the 'off', as he chatted with the communications officer who was showing him the latest batch of messages. 'It looks as if we're in for our first smell of blood. Here, look at these, Pascoe,' and he nodded at the communications officer.

Trevellion read the signals, all transmitted within the last hour. The Carrier Striking Force, having shielded the Canadian convoy by placing itself between it and the enemy's Strike Group was due west of the Azores and capable of protecting all the convoys which were now half-way across. BO–EU 2 and PH–LH 4 were entering the enemy submarine zones, which was the reason, Trevellion assumed, why the Soviet Strike had dramatically turned to the eastward, instead of getting in among the convoys. It was steering to pass north of the Azores and was thus leaving the first attacks on the convoys to the SSNs. The American admiral commanding the Carrier Striking Force had been proved right by waiting to engage the enemy ... but the crunch could not be far off now.

'You won't like the next signal, Pascoe,' Druce said. 'That's why I want to see you.'

Trevellion read and re-read the message. During the Allies' counter-attacks on the Soviet SSNs which had so badly mauled the Med-bound convoy, the ASW helicopter losses had been surprisingly grievous; over a third had been struck by unidentified missiles. Trevellion met the admiral's sharp eyes.

'Well?' Druce prompted.

'They must be using a sub-surface weapon, sir: Anvil ... unpleasantly similar to our *Icarus* incident.'

'Did your Lynx pick up anything before she was fired on?'

'Nothing, sir. Afterwards, the pilot (he's SPLOT in this ship, sir) remembered noticing a circular bulge on the surface, just before he was hit.'

'We should never have stopped research.' Druce thumped his fist against the display table. 'We're paying for it now, of course. Your pilot saw nothing else?'

'No,' Trevellion replied. 'But the incident forced us to produce our new tactics, sir. We assumed that the attacking submarine had the ability to strike at the hunting choppers.'

'It's tough on the squadron,' Druce said, 'How's it making out?'

'They're flat out, as you know, sir. The Sea Kings are working in threes now, one being guard cab against Anvil. But the new tactic keeps the crews and the hard-pushed engineers at it round the clock.'

'We'll soon see whether you've found the right solution, Pascoe. Your guard cab should be busy if the Soviets try the same ploy on us. Their ssns aren't far off now.'

The studied the charts together, Druce's stubby finger stabbing at the two red lines A and B which were drawing close to one another – less than eighty miles apart now.

'The Nimrods confirm our appreciation, Pascoe. Line A seems to have stopped its eastward drift: they're waiting for us to clear them, I reckon. Let's get up to the northward. That'll make things easier for *Valiant* and at the same time will put pressure on the enemy.'

'While waiting for the convoy to overhaul them, sir?'

'They'll let the Canadians roll over them,' Druce said, 'while line B attacks from ahead.' The admiral glanced at his flag captain. 'You'd do that, wouldn't you, Pascoe?'

'I'm not a submariner,' Trevellion said. 'And they're probably being controlled from Moscow.'

15

Sea King 833, 16 April. Hob Gamble never heard the bugle call: the first he knew of action stations was a breathless Aircrewman Osgood banging on his cabin door:

'They sounded off five minutes ago, sir. We're waiting in the briefing-room.'

'I'll be up.'

Hob rolled from his bunk, whipped on his sweater and overalls, and jammed on his flying-boots. Struggling with the zips, he began stumbling for'd and up the decks to the briefing-room. The ops officer had already dismissed the crews.

'Sorry, sir,' Hob said. 'Never heard the call.'

'Okay, Gamble. You're only just in from the dawn sortie.' He smiled grimly. 'I've told Peterson to repeat the detailed brief to you. They're waiting for you up top.'

'Thanks.' Hob glanced at the met. board: wind south-west, force eight, cloud-base twelve hundred feet. As he turned to go, the ops officer checked him: 'You still have unrestricted discretion on the use of NDBs, Gamble. But keep your ears open – ASW Group Yankee, down south, has counter-attacked SSN patrol lines with NDBS. First reports are optimistic – nine Soviet boats confirmed sunk, so goodness knows how many more possibles or damaged. The Soviets may come up at any moment on the hot line and say they've had enough of nuclear reprisals. NDB policy remains the same: *not* to be used if the enemy reverts to conventional warheads.'

Hob hurried from the room and found his crew waiting for him by the screen door opening on to the flight deck. He signed for his cab and they were off once more, hungry, tired and feeling like zombies. In the air again, they watched Old Fury sliding away beneath them, swiftly diminishing to the size of a toy boat as 833 and her two consorts, 822 and 817 (all NDB armed) climbed for height. The other flight of three Sea Kings was already on its opening heading and making for its first Jez lay. Hob watched the old carrier, seven miles astern now as she broke away from *Oileus* after the RAS: Mother was topped up with fuel. A light jackstay transfer was laid on for tomorrow when she'd be taking in stores and beer – but the serious problem was ammunition supply. Only two more NDBs were carried in *Oileus*; main stocks were in *Resurgent* who, hauled out of retirement and with only sixteen knots, was flogging up the Irish sea to rendezvous with the Force later when it turned for Fair Isle.

'You have control, Grog.'

'I have control.'

Hob handed the cab over to Grog. He was proving a reliable front-line pilot: what he lacked in experience he was making up with keenness. The crew was welding together. They were lucky to have an aircrewman as steady as Osgood: not many men would have retained their cool under the stress he was suffering at the moment, but he seemed to have put his personal problems behind him now that the war was hotting up.

'Hey, you up front!'

Dunker was disgustingly cheerful this forenoon: he was Dip Boss and responsible for the operation of the flight, but he seemed never to tire despite the considerable load that all the observers carried. The tactical battle was theirs. 'The outer screen ought to be coming up ahead soon,' Dunker called.

The weather and visibility were better up here: at sea-level a gale was blowing, the sullen clouds scudding across the wind-lashed ocean. It seemed such a short time since they had been out on their last sortie, watching the dawn come up. To be hauled out again so soon could point to only one conclusion.

'Not likely to see anything, are we, Dunker?'

'Depends on the outer screen's luck,' the observer said. 'Over the UHF they sound pretty busy.'

'What's going on?'

'Active vectacs – 831's hot. They're right among 'em: Charlies and Echos...'

Hob listened in on the net. Enemy line B was being methodically localized. The pity was that there were not enough Nimrods to go around. The RAF was stretched beyond its limits: the Russians were concentrating on shooting the unprotected

LRMP aircraft from the sky. These fifty-odd Nimrods were the Navy's first-line ASW defence and more Nimrods were essential if the submarine menace was to be contained before the SSNs struck. Hob, peering through 833's cockpit, wondered how much longer the Nimrods could hold out. The RAF had been magnificent, hounding down and localizing the possible contacts. Without Nimrod Tango, line A, the enemy's first SSN attack line less than forty miles ahead, would never have been flushed.

'Hob,' Dunker shouted suddenly. '*Valiant*'s failing to come up for her routine call. Force A's checking with the commodore, but she could have been attacked by our outer screen.'

The two pilots glanced at each other: this risk was always there when the Force operated with one of its own submarines. *Valiant*'s wardroom were drinking partners and a bloody good lot.

'You certain?' Hob asked. 'How can they be *sure*, Dunker?'

'Listening in on the chat,' Dunker said. 'There's been a balls-up on the IFF with 821 apparently. In the panic she fired her fish, without waiting for positive identification. The outer screen's claiming three enemy kills.'

It all seemed so unreal, up here, flying to their screening position forty miles ahead of *Furious*. 833, 822 and 817 were the NDB carriers on this inner screen; the other flight on Mother's starboard bow was torpedo-armed, except for its Dip Boss, 815, who carried an NDB. In minutes, Dunker would be telling Hob to lose height for the first Jez lay, a straight line-barrier between the estimated position of the enemy's line A and Old Fury. The outer screen of Sea Kings, all six torpedo-carriers, had moved on from line A over an hour ago to the enemy's line B where brisk action was now being joined. The outer screen had gone 'active' even when dealing with line A: so Dunker, the senior observer on the inner screen, was remaining passive to catch line A bending. 815 and her flight were already on their first Jez, down at eight hundred feet and below cloud-level.

The Nimrod and the outer screen assessment was nine-plus SSNs at line A – a much lower number than that proposed at the briefing. The picture was coming rapidly into focus, showing the enemy deploying from three directions: ahead, and on either bow of the approaching convoy. If the SSNs attacked, they had a wide front with which to contend: the commodore had opened out and dispersed his columns to stretch over thirty-six miles. Force Q was closing at speed, full electronic countermeasures being provided by *Furious* and her escort.

The convoy, conforming with Force Q, was at battle stations – not only was the ether charged with conflicting frequencies, but the cacophony from the foxer decoys must be deafening the enemy sonar operators for miles around in the waiting submarines. Hob's flight was dead ahead of the carrier, whence the threat was expected. 815 was ten miles to the east, to deal with attacks down the MLA.

'Hob!' Dunker called. 'They're into a nuke dead ahead, on line B.' But his whoop of delight was suddenly cut short. '*God* – something's happening to the guard cab.' Hob waited, meeting Grog's glance.

'Anvil.' Dunker swore. 'Something's shot her out of the sky. *Oh, Christ* ...'

Over the looped communication they listened to the death throes of 831, the guard cab on the westward flank of the outer screen. She was tumbling like a burning torch into the raging seas.

'Ready, up front?' Dunker snapped curtly. 'Take her down –'

But Dunker never completed his sentence. 815 was crackling out an enemy report: the SSNs in line A were reversing course and doubling back. HE from the Jez field was giving thirty-plus knots for three nukes – and all were belting back along reciprocal courses towards the convoy. The relative closing speed was over fifty knots.

'*Flash – flash – flash* ...' The call was going out in plain. The admiral, out on the north-west flank, was turning at speed to intercept on the convoy's north-western flank.

'Scrub the Jez,' Dunker called. 'The HCO's taking us over.' There was a pause and he took charge of the two flights. In seconds they had turned and then all six choppers were charging south-westwards.

'Heading 190°,' Dunker ordered. '815's ahead of us but they're moving out to the southward to cover the north-east flank.'

'What's up?' Hob asked, steadying the cab on the new heading.

'We're to lay a Jez barrier between the convoy and line B, just outside their missile firing range.' Thank God, Hob thought, their Bear formations have been broken up by the RAF off Shetland – or we'd be in a ripe old mess, countering their Echo IIS' SS-N-12 missiles. The SSNS could already have opened fire 250 miles away, from below the horizon.

'Do we go active as soon as we pick 'em on Jez?' Hob asked.

'We're to drop NDBS ahead of the nukes to make them break off their attacks. We're ready in the back.'

'Are the Harriers clear?' Hob asked. 'You've checked with Mother?'

'Affirmative,' Dunker replied. 'They're being held on the up-threat side, waiting for Bears or Badgers.'

'So we should be left with the Charlies,' Hob murmured to himself. 'With their SS-N-7s, they can fire from horizon-range.' The Charlies were presumed to have organic control of their cruise missiles, so the enemy nukes *must* be destroyed or diverted before they reached their firing positions twenty-five miles from the convoy. Their missiles could be fired from dived which rendered detection of the submarine more difficult.

Hob felt the anxiety gnawing at him: he had dropped dummy NDBS only on exercises. It was a case of getting the hell out of it as soon as the bomb was on its way down.

'815 is laying now,' Dunker reported. 'Seventeen miles ahead. Stand-by to bring her down to seven hundred.'

'Ready up front,' Hob reported. 'All set in the back?'

If 815's flight picked up a contact, perhaps her torpedoes would be sufficient to do the trick? Perhaps the enemy boats would lose their nerve and sheer away, knowing that the noise they were making was suicidal? Hob could hear Dunker and Oz checking their final settings. Osgood had latched on quickly and was gaining confidence with every sortie. Grog had finished his checks.

'Pre-dip checks completed,' Hob reported over the intercom.

'Okay – bring her down,' Dunker said. 'Seven hundred feet.'

'Here we go,' Hob called. 833 swooped downwards, followed on either side by the other two helos. They were keeping in close touch with their Dip Boss for when they went active. Hob could feel the tension: 817 was guard cab for this sortie – though the precaution had not saved the guard in the outer screen. As they passed over 815's flight, they heard them busy with their first Jez, their procedures and reports brisk and tense while they continued with their passive Jezebel tracking.

'They're hot,' Dunker said. 'Possibly two nukes.'

833 flew on to take up the ordered position in their sector, twelve miles west of 815, and thirty-seven miles from the advancing convoy which was now maintaining a continuous Sea Harrier patrol; Soviet air reconnaissance had been averted for the moment, but the convoy was still within range of Cuba.

'Bloody marvellous sight from here,' Grog commented. 'Look, Hob: even while they're altering course, they're keeping good station.'

Hob stared down at the eighteen ships battling their way through the gale: from this height, the newt-shapes were being smothered by the breaking seas while they punched onwards, trying to maintain their twenty-two knots. The MAC ships were the last in the three central columns and it was interesting to see the escorts keeping the convoy together, though the columns had now opened out to nine miles and the distance between ships increased to eight. In this anti-nuke disposition, the convoy was covering an ocean area of almost nine hundred square nautical miles.

'Seven-two miles from the commodore,' Dunker reported.

'Seven-fifty feet,' Grog monitored as they lost height, '... seven-thirty.'

'Come right,' Dunker ordered. 'New heading, two-six-oh. Stand-by to drop one sonobuoy.'

'Ready,' Osgood reported.

'Seven hundred,' Hob snapped. 'Speed ninety.'

'*Drop – drop – drop!*' Dunker's voice was tense. At thirty knots, the Soviet Charlies were covering the ground ...

'815's conducting a vectac,' Dunker yelled. 'They're firing torpedoes and the others are hot!' Hob and Grog were waiting impatiently up-front when the observer cut in again:

'Number two, *drop – drop – drop!*'

As the cab flew down her heading, Hob spotted the first sonobuoy splashing into the sea, then sliding away beneath his starboard quarter. Four and a half minutes later, the line of buoys had been laid. Almost immediately, Osgood was calling: '*I'm hot!* Bloody hell – I'm swamped by them.' He was slapping out the print-outs, while Dunker threshed away at his display.

'They're bloody mad,' Dunker cried excitedly. 'Oz's got four, possibly five on the plot.' There was a pause while Hob hauled the cab round to starboard. 'Stand by the ball,' Dunker ordered.

'Ready for first dip,' Hob said.

'For Pete's sake, Oz – chuck the Jez! Stand by the ball.' If the moment had not been so tense, Hob would have enjoyed the trauma going on in the back.

'Stand by to mark dip,' Dunker called. 'Left, full FCS. Mark dip, left.' Hob decreased his speed to ninety knots and lost height, turning into the wind.

Checking his doppler ground speed, he asked Grog:

'Ground speed?'

'Eighty.'

'Roger. We're into the wind. Engage down.'

'Engaged,' the second pilot answered.

Hob waited, counting the seconds, monitoring the controls, trying to relax as the automatic system took them from ninety knots at two hundred feet down to zero speed at forty feet. And below him, where the waves hurled themselves in confusion, the white spume blowing from the crests just below the cab, he could picture the enemy nukes, forging onwards at five hundred feet in the serene waters of the deeps as, minute by minute, they approached their missile firing positions. This bloody descent was taking eternity – Dunker should have ordered a 'modified'.

Then they were in the hover, as the doppler gauge showed by its crossed hairs. They checked that they were into wind, an easy job today with this gale blowing.

'Heading 235°,' Grog called. 'I've got thirty-five knots on my ASI.'

The peto heads were matched when Hob jerked open his window. 'No wind,' he called. He was forced to use full torque with the heavy load they were carrying. If anything went wrong at this height, they'd go straight in. Though this was hardly the moment, he had better remind them:

'If anything happens we'll go in – no question about it: we're too heavy.'

'Right,' Grog said quietly, his eyes on the curling seas ahead of them.

'Roger,' Dunker called. 'We've got the message.'

They checked the Ts and Ps, the attitude, the doppler and the trimming. Hob tried to relax as the system took over completely: 'First dip checks complete.'

Dunker was repeating Grog's order:

'Lower the body. All round sweep, axis 340°. High frequency, scale eight.'

'Roger,' Osgood called. 'Fifty feet . . .' The ball was on its way down.

'Switch to cable,' Hob ordered. The sensitive device took charge, automatically keeping the helicopter vertically over the sonar transmitter.

'One hundred feet,' Osgood called. 'Transmitting.' At last they were pinging. Less than two minutes elapsed, then Hob glanced at Grog who nodded, then grinned.

'Sonar contact 355°,' Dunker cried. 'Tack forty.'

'Crumbs! That was quick,' Hob reacted. 'You sure?'

'Certain,' Dunker called. 'No need to have another look.'

'What sort of confidence?'

'Definitely a submarine at speed: it's got twenty-eight knots closing doppler.' The observer could not conceal his excitement as he warned the other cabs.

'*Flash – flash – flash!* This is 833. Sonar contact 355°, range four zero. Contact firm. 833 – out.'

Dunker desperately needed time to achieve his active sonar tracking. The other two helicopters would be raising their sonars and be preparing to join their Dip Boss. Then Dunker was talking again to them:

'833. Sonar contact 350°, range three zero. Tracking 190°, speed twenty-eight. 822, 817, join me. Execute Plan Corral. 833 – over.'

But, as 822 acknowledged, 817 came in with another Flash Report. Before he had finished, *Furious* was cutting in. When Dunker had finished with the HCO, his voice was tense:

'822, 817,' he summoned on the UHF net. 'Execute Plan

Scorch. Height one thousand feet. Line of bearing 260° from Dip Boss. Distance interval six thousand. 833 – out.'

'Let's get the bastards,' Hob yelled. 'Raise the body.'

'Raising the body . . . eighty . . . sixty . . .' Grog said, switching from cable to doppler.

'Get that body in!' Hob couldn't contain his impatience. The attackers would be within missile range in minutes, if they weren't already coming up to firing depth.

'Body housed and latched,' Osgood called.

'Ready,' Dunker rapped. 'Execute Scorch: modified FCS, Hob. Heading 190°.'

'Engage up,' Hob ordered.

'Engaged,' was Grog's reply, cool as an ice cube.

While Hob waited for the machine to reach ninety knots and a height of two hundred feet, when he could take over pilot control by releasing the cyclic, he heard Dunker vectoring 822 and 817 to their dropping positions. They were already in station on their line-of-bearing and were opening out.

At two hundred feet Hob took over manually and turned the helicopter 45° left to her new heading. 'Heading 190°,' he called to Dunker. 'Speed ninety. Confirm height . . .'

'Dropping height, one thousand. Exit speed, maximum safe.'

'Roger.' Hob needed no prompting. He was giving her full torque at the moment, but if they were to avoid the burst area, they had to get to hell out of it. Exit speed was more vital than height.

'Ready in the back,' Dunker shouted. '822 and 817 in position. *Stand by to drop!*' he called to the other two cabs. He was working flat-out in the back, monitoring 822 and 817 on his radar display, checking his position, talking to Mother: in all their calculations, wind direction was vital.

'Four hundred feet,' Hob called. 'Eighty knots.'

His gloved fingers on the cyclic, his eyes fixed on the radalt, he and Grog were steady now, concentrating on what they had to do. No one yet knew for sure what an NDB could do to the dropping vehicle.

'This is 833,' Dunker radioed to his consorts. '822, 817, stand-by to drop. Exit heading 230°, acting independently. 833 – out.'

'822: *roger.*'

'817: *roger.*'

'Nine hundred feet . . .' Hob reported. '105 knots.'

He peered upwards, beneath the lip of the windscreen: the rotors would soon be scraping cloud base. They were prepared with their oxygen, in case they were forced to fly through the nuclear cloud. 'Check doors and windows,' Hob ordered, pinching shut his own side.

'Shut in the back,' Osgood reported.

'One thousand feet,' Hob said, seconds later. '110 knots.'

Dunker's voice crackled:

'This is Dip Boss. *Drop – drop – drop.*'

Hob felt the aircraft lurch forwards as the bomb was released from its carrier. His stomach turned over as he pushed the cyclic forward, then gave her everything he dared. The bomb was fitted with a delayed-action device, each NDB's safety delay being staggered to avoid counter-mining. How far could Hob push his cab in ninety seconds? Two miles, two and a half?

'Give me the seconds,' he snapped at Grog.

Racing from the drop datum point, Hob pushed his cab at full torque along the exit heading up-wind, so that the nuclear cloud could drift downward, away from them. He had deliberately taken her up, beyond the ordered height, so that he could take her out downhill. He'd pushed her up to the limits – a failure now and they'd be caught in the middle of the monstrous thing.

'Seventy-four – seventy-five,' Grog was counting.

They were well below the cloud-base. Hob could see the western flank of the convoy, water-beetles. It was up to Mother to warn them.

'Ninety seconds,' Grog called.

Dunker came in: '822 and 817 are –'

'*My God!*' Grog interrupted. He was pointing through his window.

Hob strained his body against his harness. At first he could see nothing from beneath the starboard wheel-float but the gale-lashed seas streaked white by tails of foam, but as he watched, the surface of the sea astern of them heaved ponderously upwards in a gigantic circle two miles across, like the domed top of a giant soufflé. This monstrous cupula humped, became slowly convex; boiled, then from its convoluted centre, burst open. The sea was flung apart, like the crater of a volcano spewing outwards. Then, sluggishly at first, the maëlstrom foamed and swirled to collapse in upon itself in one enormous whirlpool, sucking the periphery into its vortex.

The sea was metamorphosed into vapour, clouds of steam spewing upwards like a grotesque magnification of a spurting hot-water geyser. And then the vast hump began to subside while the mushroom of steam and water vapour, slowly at first, then more rapidly, soared upwards. Suddenly, the daylight behind the helicopter dimmed: the stalk was shooting through the cloud-base, only a few miles behind them.

No one spoke, forgetting their own survival while mesmerized by this shocking thing. But now another, then another cloud was billowing from the explosions of the other two NDBS.

'Keep going,' Dunker said over the intercom. 'The longer we're on this heading, the better.'

'Roger,' Hob said. 'I could feel sorry for them. Nothing can survive that. Do we stay at this height, Dunker?'

'Affirmative. Let's get out wide on the convoy's port quarter. We *must* have put paid to any attack from this quarter.'

Hob kept 833 going. They must be six miles from the nearest ship in the convoy and would soon be able to rejoin Mother. The convoy was steering down-wind, going great guns with the sea under its skirts and with the impetus of the poisoned clouds following it. It was running from the nor'-westerly submarine threat, but would soon be mixing it with the other flankers if it didn't turn back to its MLA ... Strange that they had not heard from 815 yet: she had probably been thrown by our salvo of NDBS.

'New heading,' Dunker called. 'Three –'

He never finished his sentence. There was a shout from Grog and, as Hob turned, the cab jumped, flailing, tumbling from the sky.

'*God!*' Grog cried. 'Look – missiles!'

Down below Hob saw two electric-blue flashes, then the awful trademark shooting upwards. The cab fell sideways, wrenched from its pilot's hands, as it spiralled towards the sea.

16

SS Ungava Bay, 16 April. Captain Ginger Ducrois, Master Mariner and Quebecois, leaned against the for'd rail of his bridge and gazed down the rows of boxes stacked four high from *Ungava Bay*'s main deck. The loading may have been efficient, but only by a hair's breadth did it not interfere with a clear vision ahead. He was loathe to leave his bridge. He'd been all his life at sea, had learned to heed that tightening, that inner tension. There was no other description for this instinct that set the alarm bells ringing inside him, clanging the warning of imminent danger. The phenomenon had happened three times in his life, and each time he had heeded the omen.

Still hesitating to leave the bridge for his sea-cabin abaft the radio office, Ducrois wandered out to the port wing of his modern bridge. He was glad to feel the wind blowing through his thinning hair; he refused to concede the dreary fact, but wondered whether he'd be totally white before this lot was over. So far, so good, but things were hotting up. The commodore had handled the show pretty well up to now: that turn to starboard had been a masterly effort, though the old girl on his port bow in the northern column, *Emma Rose*, had swung too far and was still trying to regain station.

'What's the commodore flying?' Ducrois shouted through the wing door at his officer of the watch. He glanced at the bridge clock below the ship's head repeater: 1242. 'You should have spotted that hoist – '

As he spoke he was pulled up sharply by a curious boom behind him, away to the northward. He felt a sudden pressure on his ears. He turned round and, rooted to the deck, saw the horizon slowly take on a monstrous hump, some eight miles away. Three choppers were flying fast to the westward.

Instinctively he crouched to gain the dubious safety of his bridge screen.

'Hit the deck!' he yelled. 'They're using nuclear stuff to winkle out the subs!'

Before he could stand up again there were two more blasts and subsequent shock waves. He waited for a few seconds, then hauled himself to window level. On the same bearing to westward he could still see the three choppers, mere dots as they streaked from 'ground zero'. They were barely in time, for the stalk of the first mushroom was forming swiftly, followed by the others. At the cloud-base the first mushroom was flattening out as the water vapour and filth shot upwards. Glancing back at the convoy, which seemed remarkably unaffected, he remembered the commodore's flag hoist.

Ducrois grabbed his binoculars and tried to read the flags – the hoist was edge-on and difficult to distinguish. The top flag of the long string was dark and rectangular: there could be an emergency turn on the way. At 1245 it was time to alter, if they were to evade the other submarine threat.

'Warn the chief,' he told the officer of the watch. 'Come to stand-by; I'll be manoeuvring shortly.'

But the young officer wasn't listening. Instead he was pointing across the port quarter. At first Ducrois thought that he was indicating the tumbling chopper on the horizon – an unnerving sight – but then the captain noticed that the officer of the watch's binoculars were trained further to the right. The chap's lips moved, but no sound came. Then Ducrois saw it.

Where the NDB had detonated, the ocean had humped to form a line of breaking seas lifting high above the horizon. As he watched, the surface hillock grew into a mountainous range, a vertical cliff of raging seas. It was advancing at an incredible speed, its silver crest stretching for miles, the wave-height increasing with every second that passed. Ducrois heard the distant roar as the confusion of the seas from the three explosions intensified.

The maëlstrom was still several miles away but would be upon the defenceless *Ungava Bay* within minutes. Ducrois held his breath as first one ship, then another and another, floated slowly up the slopes of the approaching wall of water. One by one, they were lifted, poised on the foaming crests on their beam-ends, then sucked over the summit to disappear.

'Hard-a-starboard,' he bellowed. 'Slow both engines.'

He jumped to the engine console himself, shouting at the engineer of the watch. He slithered back to the compass, shoved the paralysed officer from the pelorus. He disconnected the auto-pilot and grasped the mini-wheel himself. He left the bridge island for an instant, the wheel still hard over to check the swing as he tried to align her stern with the approaching onslaught.

As he watched, farther aft and almost astern, there was an electric flash, its glare blinding him temporarily. The thunder of the on-rushing freak wave was smothered by a blast of rushing air; the ship trembled her full length as the glass in the windows shattered in thousands of pieces. Ducrois flinched from the blistering heat, recoiled at the hammer blow of the shock wave, and gasped as the vacuum sucked at his lungs and hurled him to the deck. He dragged himself to the pelorus. He stood up, took off the wheel and met the swing as the first breakers began hissing about the ship.

Then he saw the flickering, orange light: the whole of the after part – her poop deck and the accommodation quarters – was ablaze, the paint sizzling, the stench choking his lungs as the flames were fanned by the rushing wind from the surface explosion. He could think only of survival – of keeping his ship stern-on to the monstrous sea now gripping *Ungava Bay*.

The pandemonium was overwhelming, as the sheer cliff of water surged upon the puny ship. *Ungava Bay* lurched, floundered; then, her stern lifting, Ducrois watched her bows being driven downwards as the stupendous power of the sea lifted the stern of the forty-thousand-ton ship up the slopes of the oceanic valley. He had to brace against the bow-down angle as she slid from under him; he clung to the wheel, as she lurched beam-on to the giant rollers.

The rectangle of the port bridge door, where the sky had been, darkened, transformed into a dark-green world. Millions of tons of water thundered upon the ship, but he felt her deck lifting beneath him, his heart coming into his mouth as *Ungava Bay* climbed higher and higher. She hung there at the crest, poised interminably it seemed, between wind and water. Then suddenly, the stern was slipping away, swooping down into the trough on the other side.... The bows now were rearing up – and he wound his arms about the stem of the pelorus, to save himself from being flung backwards.

The officer of the watch was a huddled heap in the corner, the engineer nowhere to be seen. Ducrois felt the ship plunging downwards, the deck subsiding beneath him, his guts thumping his diaphragm. Ever downwards she slewed, gripped in the vortex, on the far side of the fluid mountain. The electric light had gone and the mini-wheel spun uselessly in his hands. Water spurted through the bridge door, which normally stood seventy feet above the waterline.

Slowly it dawned on him that the ship was beginning to roll rhythmically, no longer being catapulted from one side to the other, the indicator showing 25° to starboard then 15° back to port and gradually decreasing. He loosened his grasp on the compass and glanced to port to see the glorious light from the sky again. Huge seas raged past him, still of hurricane height.

He stabbed at the manoeuvring controls, but there was no response. He yelled at the officer of the watch, who was now scrabbling to his feet to stare at the television screen monitoring the engine-room:

'Rudder's jammed at starboard twenty. Where the hell's the power?'

'Sorry, sir. The automatic cut-out's operated. The chief's on his way up, but all electrical power's gone.'

'Officer of the Watch, for Pete's sake.' Ducrois was venting his spleen on the young officer. 'Where the hell's the quarter-master?'

'Fetching me some cigarettes, sir, when it happened.'

Ducrois did not trust himself. He stomped to the front of the bridge, glared through the broken plate-glass. He drew in his breath as he took in the scene which met his eyes.

Over half the container boxes had gone: most of the outboard Samson posts and uprights had snapped off, those remaining being bent like reeds in the wind. The remaining container boxes were piled in confusion, jammed haphazardly together. Those nearest the bridge structure seemed to have suffered less but, for'd, most of the red ammunition containers had vanished. Amidships, what was left had been flung into a pile on the starboard side which accounted for the ten-degree list. Several boxes hung over both sides, held by heaven knew what, like beads on a necklace. At each roll, boxes thumped against the ship's side, the clanging reverberating throughout the ship. The scared face of the quartermaster showed in the starboard doorway of the bridge.

'Where the hell have you been?'

As the quartermaster entered, Ducrois saw a group of helicopters two miles off. They were flying across his stern, bound north-east, probably trying to find their carrier. Then the master realized that the fire was out, extinguished by the mountainous seas.

The bridge clock had stopped at 1246 and he checked his wrist-watch before going out to the wings to see for himself what damage the convoy had suffered. It was 1250 – only four minutes since that nuclear explosion. The thing must have been a submarine-launched missile with a nuke warhead: it must have been fired from the other side where the other chopper flight was still operating. He strode briskly across his bridge and stepped outside on to the starboard wing.

He thought he had had enough surprises for the afternoon, but he counted five more mushroom clouds, dark and sinister, spreading across the sky above the eastern horizon: the missiles must have been deceived by our ECM because the bursts were wide. They had obviously detonated during *Ungava*'s minutes of near-disaster, for he had not heard the explosions nor felt their pressure waves.

He began to count the ships from this side. As he began to check the numbers, a sixth hump erupted on the horizon, to the left of another flight of Sea Kings, to the eastward. His stomach heaved; he felt nauseated. *Ungava Bay* could never survive another ordeal like the last.

He followed the closest flight of helicopters, saw them bank steeply, turning away from the nuclear cloud: those boys bore a charmed life. 1252: it was about time the mate made his report ... Ducrois counted twelve ships in all, most of them still steaming, some circling like *Ungava Bay*, shaken or damaged.

But there was no sign of those three in the port column adjacent to his... The tail-end Charlies in his and the commodore's column were both on fire. One of them was a trooper and he turned his face away, feeling sick, as he watched them trying to lower boats while a frigate nosed beneath the trooper's transom. It was a gallant effort, but she could only damage herself in this weather. He hurried back into the bridge to check on the other side. Through the shattered windows he could see another escort racing through the seas, spray shooting masthead-high as she butted into the swell – but pygmy stuff compared to what *Ungava Bay* had just endured.

'Captain, sir.'

He turned towards the mate who, at the back of the bridge, was waiting for the chief by the screen door.

'I'm trying to get the turbos going, sir,' the chief puffed. 'The port diesel generator has a fractured mounting, but we're starting number one now: that should restore lighting and give us back our hydraulics.'

'Fifteen feet of plating's gone on the port quarter, sir,' the grey-faced mate said, 'just above the water-line.' He wiped the sweat from his forehead. 'Our geigers are crackling like crickets, so we'll have to decontaminate before we can get at the damage. Water's pouring into the pump room where a plate's stove in. The sooner the chief can give us power on the main line the better.'

Ducrois was master of himself and his ship again. This emergency was something he understood, a problem requiring seamanship and engineering skills.

'Okay. What about the main engines, chief?'

The overweight engineer officer shook his head: 'Boiler feed's gone, sir – but nothing we can't fix. The boys are on to it. I'll have to look at the turbines. I'm worried about the port ahead turbine: may have fractured feet. If all's well, I shouldn't be too long with the starboard engine.'

'Any idea?'

'Two hours, sir.' He shook his head again, his lugubrious face expressionless. 'That's being optimistic.'

The master pointed for'd through the windows:

'We've got to square that off before I can get under way

again. You've got two more hours, you and every available hand, while we wait for the chief. I can't risk knocking a hole in her.'

'We're a long way from Oslo, sir.'

'And it's going to be lonely out here,' Ducrois said, 'on our Jack, a sitting duck in the middle of the Soviet submarine packs.' He glanced at them both:

'Turn out the lifeboats, gentlemen,' he said. 'Just in case. Leave 'em on the gripes.'

17

HMS Furious, 16 April. Trevellion heard the screening curtains of the ops room rustling behind him.

'833 flight landing-on now, sir.'

Wings held the curtain for him and together they went outside to the passageway alongside Flyco where they could look down upon the flight deck. Trevellion heard the pipe, 'Romeo section to right, aft is out of bounds, repeat out of bounds.' For the past hour the ship had been at full nuclear biological chemical defence.

'They *must* have been through the nuclear cloud, sir. We tracked them but though they did their best to dodge the bursts, they must have been close.'

The contaminated water fell like rain, Pascoe knew, and he did not see how 833 and her flight could have missed being drenched by the stuff. The carrier had managed to stay clear of the wind path and the dosimeters were still showing negative radio-activity.

833 was landing on spot $7\frac{1}{2}$ which had already been sprayed with the decontamination agent. It was as well that they had exercised this drill so often, because the aircrewman opening the door and jumping out was Osgood, brand new to the game. Because of the contamination risk no one could help, so the aircrewman and observer had to secure the lashings themselves. 817 and 822 were hovering off the ship's port quarter, waiting while 833 was washed down with the special foam. The decontamination squad and the PMO, in their disposable plastic suits, were standing by while Osgood finished his lashings. Then Osgood was standing back and giving a thumbs-up: the pilot shut down the power.

The crew tumbled out, were frisked by the PMO with his dosimeter; then, in single file, they hurried along the treated carpet which led across the flight deck to the screen door opening into the ship's citadel.

The decontamination squad was moving in, grotesque in anti-gas respirators and plastic suits. Two of them were scrambling across the Sea King to fill in all intakes before the spraying began. Trevellion watched them, depressed by this foul brand of warfare, until the second wash-down with sea water was finished. The handlers moved in and she was trundled to spot 4. 817 was approaching, crabbing sideways in response to the batsman.

'Thanks, Wings,' Trevellion said. 'The training's paying off. Let me know when the aircraft will be airworthy again.'

'Aye, aye, sir,' Craddock said. 'The machines will keep going longer than the crews at this rate. It's been non-stop for the past thirty-six hours.'

'Yes, Wings, I know,' Pascoe said quietly. 'Ease up all you can for the rest of today: I'll be needing every machine you can give me once we're past Rockall. We'll be into the bottle-neck then.'

'ETA Rockall, sir?'

'2300 tonight, 0300 tomorrow morning for the convoy, if it can maintain its speed – depends on the stragglers.'

'How much rest I can give the crews depends on your screening policy, sir. I've got only one flight in the air at the moment.'

'I'll let you know as soon as I've seen the admiral. Use this lull, Wings, to arm every aircraft you can get into the air.'

'NDBs, sir? We've only two left. The nearest stock is flogging up the Minches in *Resurgent*.'

'I can't tell you yet. I hate the bloody things.' Trevellion glanced at his senior airman. 'But it's the men who are our limiting factor now: we've already lost two crews to Anvil. Did Guard Cab Two sight anything before she was shot down?'

'Dip Boss said he heard them, but their shouting was unintelligible: he thinks they'd picked up a small echo on their radar from the sub-contact. "Firm," they reported before communication died.'

'We're four crews down altogether,' Trevellion said. 'And supposing these boys have been contaminated?'

Craddock shook his head. 'They'll keep flying, sir. Whatever the PMO does to 'em.'

Trevellion left the after corner of the bridge and slowly retraced his steps to the ops room. He knew, as they all did, that the only way to save a man contaminated by nuclear fall-out, was to carve out the contaminated flesh . . .

Trevellion paused outside, tried to shake off the astonishingly fierce hatred he felt for this utterly inhuman form of warfare. 'Love thine enemy,' his Bible reminded him frequently, but what about loving anti-Christ? Trevellion stooped and pushed through the curtains into the gloom of the ops room.

Druce was hunched over the command displays. At his side the communication officer waited, message pad in hand.

'I'm considering whether to re-establish electronic silence, Pascoe,' Druce murmured. 'For the past few hours it's been to our advantage to swamp the air. But take at look at this plot.' His stubby finger prodded the small-scale chart of the Northern and Western Approaches. 'This last fracas will seem like a tea-party compared with what's to come.'

Trevellion threw himself into his command chair. He didn't speak, absorbing the mass of information which the vast ops room presented to the command. The plot and chinagraph pencil had been taken over completely by the case computer which tracked all echoes and threw them up on the displays; it even back-tracked, displaying whence ships and aircraft had come. The compartment was huge, packed with the vital visual display units which were the end-products of the search and missile radars, the identification responders, the helicopters and fighter-tracking radars, and the EW and ECM systems; thirty officers and men were always on watch. The direction officer fought the air war using his own electronics and radio frequencies. This air picture was filtered and presented on the command display but, at the moment, only three blips were showing on Trevellion's screen. The three helos were eighty miles ahead of their Jez runs, screening the Force as best they could while the squadron prepared for the next round.

'We'd better take stock,' Druce said. 'Has *Phoebe* come up with her report on *Ungava Bay* yet?'

'I'm waiting for her amplifying report, sir. Doesn't look too good.'

'Shall I ask her, sir?' the PWO, a senior lieutenant-commander asked from his display on the captain's right.

'She'll come up as soon as she can.'

Druce had despatched the frigate to help the convoy's hard-pressed team. *Phoebe*, a point-defence frigate, with her Sea Cats and Exocets, was the right escort for the stricken container ship. Though the frigate was a vital component of Force Q, *Ungava Bay* was at the core of the whole convoy, with her vital cargo of ammunition and transport for the Canadian Division.

Druce rasped:

'Five ships lost, Pascoe.' He did not look up from the display. 'And *Valiant* sunk by our own team. Where've we gone wrong, eh?'

Trevellion did not reply at once. In such a holocaust, it was impossible to analyse without knowing the details...

'How many enemy submarines d'you reckon we sank, sir?'

'Conjecture only...' Druce was jotting on the pad at his elbow. 'The advanced screen definitely killed three: *Gloucester* and *Köln* picked up survivors. 831 sighted bits and pieces of another, so that's definite.'

'And *Brazen* got a possible, sir,' the PWO added. 'She had a riser and finished off the submarine with her fish. They found nothing, but heard her breaking up at depth. And our Nimrod's confirmed a "probable" and "two possibles".'

'That's seven,' said Druce. 'What about the other thirteen supposed to be on line B?'

'The NDBs may have scared 'em, sir,' the PWO continued. 'Perhaps they let us roll over them?'

'To live another day,' Trevellion added, 'or to overhaul the convoy and attack from the rear tonight.'

'They've got the speed — faster than our escorts in this weather,' the PWO added.

'Darkness means nothing to 'em,' Druce said, 'but it makes things bloody difficult for our Sea Kings.'

'What was the score against line A?' Trevellion asked.

'815 sank one by torpedo,' the admiral said. 'Impossible to say what casualties the NDBs inflicted, but they certainly discouraged the bastards. We'll have to wait for intelligence for reliable figures — if we *ever* find out.'

'No submarine within range could survive that heat,' Trevellion said, 'so the score depends on the concentration of enemy boats. The weather didn't help them with visual sightings. They don't hang around much, do they, when our Sea Kings are in the offing?'

Druce chuckled. 'Maybe we've made our point,' he said. 'After the first salvo of nuclear missiles, 815's NDBs seems to have dissuaded them. There've been no more missile attacks, though they *must* have been within range for at least an hour.'

The communications officer interrupted at the admiral's elbow: '*Phoebe* reports that *Ungava Bay* is clearing away her damaged container boxes, sir. They've got power again and hope to free her rudder within two hours. They're making good her damaged side, but the starboard castings of her turbine feet are fractured. They won't be able to make the speed of the convoy, sir.'

The convoy was already twenty-four miles ahead of the container ship who was drifting in the centre of a hornet's nest: even if *Phoebe* stayed with her, the chance of them both being sunk was high. But if *Phoebe* remained with her, would not Force Q – and therefore the convoy – be even more at risk? Trevellion heard only the subdued voices of the operators at their work. 'We can't abandon her, sir,' he murmured.

'Catch 22,' Druce said sharply. 'Our priority is the safe delivery of the convoy. D'you think I enjoy this any more than you, captain?'

The index finger of Trevellion's bony hand pointed to the southern tip of the Outer Hebrides. 'Detach her independently with *Phoebe* to Barra, sir. She can find her way up the Minches. A pity we can't spare a pilot and observer so that she could maintain constant Lynx cover.'

Druce hesitated, then pricked off the distances with his dividers. 'She might even catch up with us if she makes the passage of the Pentland Firth . . . if we're held up.' He turned to the communications officer. 'Make it so, Derek, but show me your draft before you get it off. Repeat the message to the screen.' He turned to the PWO: 'What's the air picture give us?'

'Nothing much, sir. Half a dozen Bears north-east of Iceland, reckoned to be searching for Nimrods and to be screening the

Northern Fleet's second battle group. ACLANT's airsit suggests that the enemy is holding in reserve his main air strike of two regiments of Backfires. He'll attack when he's identified the main threat.'

'Looks uncommonly as if we're the prime target,' Druce murmured. 'The RAF will be standing-by once we're north of Rockall, but we can't depend on them – they'll have their hands full. God – how we need our own organic air, Pascoe!' The admiral was sweeping his hand across the Arctic Circle east of Iceland. 'I'm convinced the Northern Fleet's second battle group is poised here,' he emphasized. 'SATCOM reports grade two detection of surface forces here, and one of our SSN's got off a Flash Report on one of their two new battle-cruisers. We've got to weigh up the enemy's capability, Pascoe.' The admiral turned to his staff officer, operations. 'What are we up against, SOO, if we meet their battle-cruisers?'

'They're powerful ships, sir. With their 32,000 tons and nuclear power, they can hit hard: they're packed with guided missiles and can out-shoot anything we can range against them. CINCEASTLANT's Harriers confirm that they've their latest carrier with them, the fourth of the Kiev class.'

'Fifteen V/STOL and twenty choppers,' the PWO added.

'Something for our five Harriers to get their claws into,' Roderick Druce said. 'I presume the Red Air Force will draw off the RAF's fighters before they despatch their Backfires to attack us and the convoy.'

'The Backfires had a go at the Yanks off the Azores, sir. They tried to pre-empt the Carrier Striking Force, but the Yanks weren't playing this morning.'

'What d'you mean?'

'Our Carrier Striking Force is still covering *Kiev* and her Strike Group, sir. At noon today the Soviet Force was 150 miles north of Flores, tailed by US bombers; Carrier Striking Force is still shadowing 160 miles to the south. ACLANT is holding up the eastbound convoys until the battle's decided.'

'The Azores seem to be the jam in the sandwich, SOO.'

'It looks as if the enemy is trying to draw the Yanks towards the Soviets' submarine area west of Gib, sir.'

Trevellion listened in silence.

'And the sub-surface picture?' asked Druce. 'What've you got for us?' The PWO stood back and pointed out the enemy submarine dispositions. Here, in the gaps, the estimations of enemy forces were much firmer: our SSKS, Sosus, Stass and the LRMPS were seeing to that, but for how long could these gallant Nimrods continue to operate?

'The enemy boats are waiting for us, *here*, this side of the Faeroes–Shetland Gap, an iron ring from Lousy Bank to the two-hundred-metre line off the Butt of Lewis – two SSNS, probably Victors, coming down from the Iceland–Faeroes Gap; the others are on their billet, a mixed bag of eight SSKS, probably Tangos and Foxtrots.'

'Interesting,' Trevellion said. 'I wonder if you're thinking as I am, sir?' A slow grin lit up his gaunt face as he waited for Druce to reply:

'I'm with you,' Druce said. 'They're all torpedo submarines. The air boys will have first go.'

Trevellion nodded. 'That'll be the main threat tomorrow, sir, when the convoy enters its sixty-degree turn to the eastward for the Skroo and Fair Isle.'

'We'll still be in deep water, so their SSNS can also have a go,' Druce said. 'If, at the same time, their Northern Fleet's Second Battle Group makes a quick dash south – and manages to co-ordinate its threat with our turn, we'll be in for a busy evening. ETA for the convoy's turn, Pascoe?'

'1900, sir.'

'We could do with a bit of help,' Roderick Druce remarked.

'STANAVFORLANT is belting up from the south, sir,' SOO said, 'now that the French have got the Sole Banks well covered. They've lost a couple of frigates but they're cleaning up the enemy SSNS whenever they're on to a firm contact. They're not so hard-stretched with their LRMPS – their Atlantics and Neptunes don't have to cover such a vast area.'

'Yes, but the French are farther away and have just sent some of their ships round the Cape in the Indian ocean. What concerns me is our immediate defence of the convoy tomorrow. Relax to Alert Ten, captain. Your fliers have got to get some sleep or they'll be NBG for tomorrow.'

'Thank you, sir. We could do with it.' Trevellion looked up:

Craddock was standing there, the communications officer at his side. It was the first time that Trevellion had seen the suspicion of a smile on Craddock's face.

'The PMO sends his compliments, sir, because he can't leave the sick bay,' Craddock said. 'He reports that 833's flight are lucky to have got away with no radiation contamination. He's given them a jab to make sure. He'll be up to see you as soon as he's checked on the others.'

'Good news,' Druce said. 'Are they fit to fly?'

'Six hours rest, sir. They'll be fit for duty by 2300 tonight.'

'Just in time, Wings. I'll be needing every aircraft from midnight onwards.' Druce jerked from his seat and began pacing the cramped space between the displays.

'Get your heads down, all of you,' he said. 'We'll meet again at midnight. I'll signal my intentions to the escorts then.'

Trevellion climbed to his feet. 'I'll talk to the ship's company at supper, sir. Would you care to have a word?'

Druce nodded. 'Thanks, Pascoe. It's time I talked to them. The next two days will be critical.'

'Sir?' The communications officer was loath to interrupt the prowling admiral. 'Two messages, both priority,' and he handed the signal sheets across the displays.

After scanning the first, Druce grunted. '*Ungava Bay*'s under way and hoping for twelve knots. *Phoebe* gives an ETA for Barra Head, 0200 Friday.' He glanced at the track chart, pricked off the distances. 'She'll be two hundred miles astern of us, even if she goes through Pentland.'

'She's got *Phoebe*,' Trevellion said. 'And a lot can happen yet to the convoy.'

'Yes, a lot can happen. . .' Druce tailed off as he re-read the signal. He peered up at his flag captain.

'Well, Pascoe, your aviators seem to have done the trick – ' But he never finished his sentence.

'The First Sea Lord's on the blower, sir,' the communications officer interrupted. He passed over the red telephone. The others rose quietly from their seats to make themselves scarce.

'No, Pascoe, stay.' Then he was barking at the telephone: 'Sir. ASW Group Commander here. Yes, sir.' Trevellion watched Druce's face for a hint of information. 'Yes, right

131

away. Aye, aye, sir.' He handed the instrument back to the signals officer.

'That confirms it, Pascoe,' he said with a gleam in his eye. 'The Kremlin's been through on the hot line. No more nuclear missiles, providing we lay off the NDBs.' He grinned broadly. 'The Yanks down south reckon they've had a massacre too with their NDBs. An enemy nuke had only to declare herself and the bomb does the rest.'

'That's good, sir. I loathe the things.' Trevellion stroked his chin with his long fingers, in that typical gesture of his. 'The enemy will be busy re-arming tonight in the Northern Fleet's battle groups, sir. We can take off our cricket boxes – and so can the EASTLANT ships.'

But Trevellion still felt the apprehension of those around him. A conventional HE-headed missile was still a formidable weapon and could inflict terrible damage.

18

Sea King 833, 17 April. Aircrewman Osgood never saw Rockall with its colonies of gannets but, during the last of 833's Jez runs, he glimpsed the red marker lights on the rigs that were still operating the oil-wells on the edge of the Rockall Trough. He wouldn't have chosen to be working there just at the moment...

When they had debriefed from their first watch sortie, they waited for the Sea Harriers to scramble. Two Harriers were sent off to the west to discourage a group of positively identified Backfires which had been picked up by the Force's AEW Nimrod.

Osgood was trying to prevent his eyelids, as heavy as dumbbells, from closing while 833 flew through the murk again, two sorties later. Though he had snatched four hours' sleep and enjoyed an unhurried dinner of beef and spuds, which should have set him up, he still craved sleep – and the stodgy meal did nothing to stimulate him. The ordeal of existing under the cloud of a murder charge wasn't affecting his sleep one jot.

He had told them at the murder inquiry exactly what he had seen and he could do no more. Petty Officer Kotta swore until he was purple in the face that Osgood had committed the crime, but the evidence from 4N8 were mounting against the PO. Although Toastie Cole had told them very little in the inquiry, what he did let slip did Kotta no good. Being under open arrest didn't restrict Osgood, and made no difference under present conditions – the mess was going out of its way to make life easy for him. As for his pain over Gwen, he was learning to lock up his anxiety inside himself.

Dunker was putting the final touches to his plot – half an hour to go before Hob and Grog got them to their screen position sixty-five miles south-east of the radio beacon of Akraberg on Suderöe, the southernmost island of the Faeroes group. Every helo which could fly was in the air, their crews operating round the clock to protect the convoy which followed 140 miles astern of the Mother. Thank God, STANAVFORLANT had joined in the nick of time. Osgood knew that, for him at least, these next few hours would be crucial. Death had already depleted the squadron, and the present routine left him little time for feeling sorry for himself.

'Ready for the Jez?' Dunker asked. 'We'll be in position shortly.'

'All ready, sir,' Osgood responded. 'Ball's ready too.'

Osgood lapsed back into his musing as he tried to make himself more comfortable in his canvas seat. He hadn't known what he was letting himself in for when he'd transferred to the Fleet Air Arm. In less than a week he had gathered as much experience as he would in ten years of peacetime. Things had happened fast during the last forty-eight hours.

'Five minutes to go,' Dunker called.

They were almost on billet. The next few hours would see it all over for them, perhaps, as the enemy subs closed in at speed for the kill off Position Juliett. Down south, the Yanks had clobbered the Soviet Strike Group which had been menacing the convoys, so perhaps our Carrier Striking Group Two might do the same up here. The battle between the giants had taken place at dawn, 150 miles east of San Miguel in the Azores. Each side had been waiting for the other to make the first move, but at dawn the Soviet Strike Group struck. There were no details as yet, except that one of the big Soviet carriers had been sunk with heavy loss of life. The Americans had suffered too, mostly from concerted attacks from Backfires. By all accounts, it had been a bloody battle of attrition.

833 was flying in conditions which would have been beyond the limit ten days ago – force eight for the past six days, and still no sign of letting up as the tail of the equinoctials continued to create atrocious weather. But, if it hadn't been for the wind yesterday, might not all the choppers have been caught by the fall-out from the nuclear exchange?

For Osgood – and almost everyone in the ship – this was the first taste of waiting for probable extinction. Funnily enough, he felt quite calm about it, sitting in the back of Sea King 833. Calm, but he didn't relish the encounter.

'1450,' Dunker called. 'Are you ready up-front to go in? Take her down to cloud-base, Hob.'

'Roger,' Hob acknowledged. 'Tally-ho, one thousand feet.'

Osgood checked his buoys. 833 was falling out of the sky, Hob revelling in being free of restrictions. The chat ceased, each man intent on his drill. They were out here, alone but for 822 and 827, the lives of thousands of men and dozens of ships depending on their skill and resolution. 817 was guard cab this time: the lives of three chopper crews hung on her alertness against the much-feared Anvil.

19

HMS Furious, 17 April. 'The next two hours will decide the issue,' Druce said conversationally.

Trevellion fumbled in his jacket for his tobacco pouch. Methodically he pressed the tobacco into the bowl of his pipe as he watched Druce flicking his dividers across the chart.

'The Northern Fleet has to engage now if it wants to attack the convoy,' Druce remarked.

Everything depended upon when to open fire. All electronic counter-countermeasures depended upon this decision. Trevellion smiled briefly as he remembered the gunner's remark: 'Sir, our anti-missile missile has just shot itself down.' Technical intelligence was the key to all operations these days. The commander who knew most about the other side's weapons and EW would win this war. At last, official policy didn't insist that he waited for the enemy to open fire on him.

There was precious little room around the general operations plot where Druce was considering the tactical moves open to him. The GOP, being linked to the radars and computers, could predict future moves of the enemy, and, with its longer range and time scale, was a vital tool in the coming battle. Trevellion pulled at the anti-flash hood which was stifling him. It was hot, clad in anti-flash gear, but at least they weren't wearing helmets as the men in exposed positions were forced to do. Pascoe checked the ship's time against the plot: 1640.

'Consider the enemy's intentions first,' Druce said. 'I met Stukalov once: I'm not surprised he's C-in-C of their Northern Battle Fleet. Where are we at the moment, SOO?'

The staff officer, operations indicated the blue crosses on the surface of the plot, timed at 1700.

Trevellion listened in silence as the dispositions were marked off: HX-OS 1 was safely past the enemy SSN line and managing to maintain its speed of advance: the convoy should be up to its

1900 ETA in two hours time for the turn at Position Juliett towards Fair Isle. Force Q, minus *Phoebe*, with *Furious* at its centre on a continuous 'weave' zigzag, was disposed along a line of bearing 115°–295°. The Sea Kings were eighty miles ahead, flushing the enemy submarine line in the Faeroes–Shetland gap. Druce had maintained room to manoeuvre, as the convoy approached its vital turn.

'Stukalov knows what we're doing,' Druce snapped. 'He hasn't been hanging around Iceland for the past twenty-four hours for nothing: the island commander has been at "immediate alert" for the past two days!'

The staff officer, operations was indicating the Northern Fleet's track since 0100 this morning when *Furious*' Harriers had intercepted the Bears. Twenty minutes later, Stukalov had increased speed to twenty-five knots despite the appalling weather and had altered to the southward in an attempt to shake off COMSTRIGRUTWO, commanded by Rear-Admiral Boyd. But Striking Group Two had hung on and at 0900 the Russians had set course for Bill Bailey's Bank, the fishing ground west of Position Juliett.

'Where's Rosy Boyd at the moment, SOO?' Druce asked.

'Here, sir, seventy miles east of the enemy. They're both racing south on parallel courses.'

'When will Stukalov be in range of the convoy?'

'Any moment now, sir. His two battle-cruisers' SS-N-12s have a range of 250 miles, with mid-course guidance.'

'Rosy will be opening fire at any moment. Anything from EW?'

'All electronic restrictions have been lifted, sir. Both sides are jamming. The enemy's pulse rate has shifted.'

'Like an exercise, sir,' Trevellion murmured, anxious to return to his bridge. 'They'll try to co-ordinate their surface threat in one overwhelming air attack.' He turned to the HCO: 'How are our Sea Kings doing, James?'

'The picture's confirmed, sir. One Victor in the centre, two SSKs on either side. They're closing at speed but aren't clear of the restricted area yet.'

Trevellion nodded. 'Our own submariners are waiting for them – they'll be getting in their shots any time now. Once the

137

enemy boats are clear of the restricted area, our ASW helos can get cracking.'

'You're right, captain,' Druce murmured. 'We can expect the air threat to coincide. If Stukalov intends to attack during our turn at Juliett, the air threat is due at any moment.'

'It's disconcerting how they've anticipated our movements,' SOO said. 'Security's been as tight as we could get it.'

The HCO was reporting on the intercom:

'The Victor's gone up to thirty-one knots.'

Druce nodded at his flag captain:

'Here we go, Pascoe.'

'What's holding our Striking Group?' Trevellion murmured. 'It's time to break things up...'

'I don't think so. Stukalov needs to get closer. Rosy's biding his time to exploit the enemy's weakness. He'll try to break up their co-ordination.'

The direction officer was on the line:

'Four hundred plus aircraft from Leningrad threatening oil rigs and the east coast of UK. Possible targets, Rosyth and Faslane. UKADGE is being forced to react with maximum effort.'

'There's our confirmation, Pascoe,' the admiral said quietly.

The direction officer was reporting again: 'Six regiments of Backfires reported airborne from Kola. Target unknown but tracking west at height. ETA Faeroes 1750.'

Then Pascoe heard the report for which they had all been waiting: the Flash from Rear-Admiral Boyd, COMSTRIG-RUTWO.

'Battle's joined,' Druce rapped. 'Clear the air.'

Trevellion again glanced at the enemy state board.

The two new battle-cruisers (for that was what they were) were 32,000-ton ships, nuclear-powered, with thirty-four knots. They were bristling with surface-to-air and surface-to-surface missiles.

'Scramble the CAP-on-deck,' Druce ordered. 'Area of search, sectors India, Juliett and Kilo. Probable targets, Badgers and Bears.'

'All four Harriers, sir?'

'Yes, captain. Keep your second CAP-on-deck.'

Trevellion glanced at the admiral. Roderick Druce was ice-cool: move and counter-move, this was the moment for which he had been trained. An error of judgement now and catastrophe could overtake them all.

'I detest inactivity, Pascoe,' he said. 'All we can do is to wait and listen to what Rosy's up to.'

The ops room team listened in silence to the battle being joined 190 miles to the north, 110 miles nor'-nor'-west of the Faeroes. Only the murmurs of the plotting operators could be heard. Trevellion watched the two fleets converging, as he had so often done during the wargames at the Staff College.

Attacking Stukalov's powerful fleet, COMSTRIGRUTWO was superior in shipborne airpower, but was at a considerable disadvantage in surface-to-surface weaponry. Unlike the Russians, two of our fleet submarines were operating with Rosy Boyd, as well as a fast combat stores ship, an ammunition ship and a replenishment oiler.

'Wings is asking whether he should recall the Sea Kings, sir,' Trevellion said.

'When's the latest Charlie-time?' asked Druce.

'1800 – SPLOT's flight. The first of the screen is due back at 1750.'

Druce hesitated, then added quickly:

'Keep 'em at it. We'll see how things develop: they may be safer in the air, away from the mêlée.'

Trevellion felt relieved. Fuelling, even in the hover, from a carrier which was wheeling and firing her guns and missiles, was not the safest of evolutions.

'Our choppers will be clear to attack in a few minutes, sir,' the PWO chipped in. 'Distance of the nearest enemy submarine is now thirty-five miles.'

'The Victor?'

'Affirmative, sir.'

Trevellion was watching Druce closely. If the Victor (the fastest class of submarines in the world, but torpedo-armed only) wanted a crack at the convoy – or even at *Furious* – she would have to speed up. Then the Sea Kings would be able to have a go at her.

'Report from CINCEASTLANT, sir: *United* has killed an SSK at the northern end of the Faeroes–Shetland gap. Estimated four enemy submarines remaining. Our own boats are withdrawing from the area.'

'Roger,' Druce acknowledged. He turned to Trevellion. 'Send your choppers in, Pascoe,. We'll hold out a carrot to the Victor – turn away and make him chase us. That'll give your fliers a better chance.'

'Close the convoy?' Trevellion asked.

Druce nodded. It was difficult to guess what was going on in Rosy Boyd's court, but in less than an hour the first of the HX–OS 1 convoy would be into the turn. Trevellion breathed a sigh of relief: nothing nuclear yet or we would have heard from CINCEASTLANT. He spoke aloud over the line to the bridge. 'Captain – Officer of the Watch. Bring her round to starboard to 240°. Continuous weave.'

The staff officer, operations was talking rapidly, analysing Striking Group Two's action situation report: 'Rear-Admiral Boyd engaged first, sir. The Phantoms have gone in: seventy-five per cent estimated losses. One hit on the farthest battle-cruiser, two on *Minsk*. Most of our missiles went wide – ECM, I gather. The Tomcats followed up immediately from out of the setting sun. *Leningrad* is stopped and on fire, but their SS-N-12s began hitting in spite of our ECM. *Kennedy*'s hit, her speed reduced, amplifying report to follow.' He glanced across at Druce. 'Communications bad, sir; full ECM from both sides.'

'What's CINCEASTLANT up to?' Druce asked. 'Nothing from him yet?'

Pascoe glanced at the long range plot. Flag Officer First Flotilla was patrolling ninety miles north-east of Muckle Flugga, where he was serving a dual purpose: protecting the northern oilfields and flushing out the line of six SSKs disposed in an arc north of Shetland. *Illustrious* had scrambled her Harriers; one had shot down a Badger guiding for Stukalov's fleet.

The AWO (Air) cut in:

'Here they come, sir,' he said calmly. '120-plus Backfires, estimated in regimental deployment, sir. Range 540, bearing zero-eight-zero, heading two-six-zero – tracking.'

Trevellion heard the fighter controller vectoring his four Harriers towards the approaching armada.

'UKADGE can't reinforce, sir: the RAF's committing its final reserve.'

Trevellion sat still. No one spoke.

'I'll bring her round, sir,' Trevellion said, meeting Druce's silent query. 'I'll take the threat bows-on.'

20

HMS Furious, 17 April. 'Air raid warning Red!'

Captain Trevellion heard the PWO's abrasive voice cutting through the low chatter in the ops room. Pascoe braced himself instinctively: no exercise, this. Whether they would be swimming shortly or not, whether the convoy was to survive, depended upon the effectiveness of the Navy's training over the past three decades. No one knew whether they had got it right: this was a different type of warfare.

Craddock was on the line:

'The first flight's Charlie-time is up, sir. They're in-flight refuelling.'

'Very good.' Trevellion was thankful that he need not worry about his helos at this moment. They would be picking up their fuel lines on the hover, remaining airborne, so that Old Fury could maintain freedom of manoeuvre: the aircraft could slip their fuel hoses instantly, while he concentrated on fighting his ship. He was glad, too, that the carrier was back with her Force, while her consorts took up their up-threat dispositions to cover the convoy. He had grown used to fighting his ship from the ops room, but he had learnt always to keep his eye on the officers of the watch. When manoeuvring, however good they were at over-riding the command decisions, they still needed watching.

'MLA 215°,' Trevellion ordered the bridge. The new course would bring the Force within eighteen miles of Position Juliett. 'Start number seven zigzag.' A sneak submarine attack still could not be ruled out.

'CAP One in contact, sir,' the fighter controller reported. 'Main threat eighty-plus Backfires; 080°, three hundred miles, height five thousand metres. Secondary threat, 085°, 360 miles from CAP One.' He added: 'They're low. Relative closing speed – Mach one decimal eight.'

Unless the encounter was head-on the Harriers had little chance of coping with these supersonic bombers.

'Tell 'em to go for the Badgers and Bears,' Trevellion ordered.

The fighter controller was on to the Harriers, hauling them off, directing them on to the enemy aircraft which could vector the missiles of the Northern Fleet on to the convoy.

'Expected time of the Harriers' encounter?' Trevellion asked.

'In seven minutes, sir: 1759.'

The quality which Trevellion valued most in Roderick Druce was his ability to leave his flag-captain alone and allow him to get on with the job, although it was good to feel Druce behind him, if help was needed. Druce must be itching to know when Trevellion was going to implement EW ...

'*Gloucester* requests simulation, sir.'

'Execute,' Trevellion snapped. So the EW team would be trying to deceive the enemy by emitting a false echo of the carrier's position, to the north westward and away from the convoy.

'Flash Report from *Gloucester* ... to all ships, sir,' the PWO said. 'Shall I start EW, sir?'

Trevellion glanced at the EW presentation on his display which was already being cluttered by enemy transmissions: the Northern Fleet could be within SS-N-12 range at any second. He glanced across at Druce who nodded imperceptibly.

'Start EW,' Trevellion rapped.

'Sea Cats ready,' the gun director, blind reported. *Furious* was in all respects ready for action and Trevellion felt the frustration slipping from him, as he concentrated on fighting his great ship.

'CAP One is engaging with Skyflash.'

The subdued cheer did them all good. The Sea Harriers were proving their worth and justifying the Navy's faith in them after so many years of scepticism.

The fighter controller was listening intently to the Harriers. He turned, his face beaming. 'Five hits, sir. All missiles fired. Returning to Mother.'

And then Trevellion heard what he had been dreading:

'The bogies are coming in, sir: fifteen in formation. CAP One requests permission to get in among 'em with their cannon.'

'Negative,' Trevellion snapped. 'Return to Mother.' He raised his bushy eyebrows and glanced at Druce.

'Scramble CAP Two,' Trevellion ordered as Druce nodded in agreement. 'Go for the Bears.'

The second combat air patrol of Harriers would be airborne within the minute, but every *second* counted now . . .

'Panther Three – Keeper,' the PWO rapped. 'Go to first alternative AWC.'

So the EW game had started, each side trying to fool the other with the code words for its frequencies.

'Liar Dice – roger,' he continued. 'Full House.'

Trevellion listened to the insane game they had played so often. They were shifting frequencies now, to fox the enemy with different air-cover frequencies. Everything depended on this, up to the final second before the missiles homed on to their targets.

'Bogies are jamming our radar, 093° from 082°,' the operator reported.

Trevellion glanced at his EW presentation at the left-hand end of the battery of displays glowing orange in the dim room: the underwater picture; the air; then the plot and, next to it, the state boards, the enemy's glowing red.

'CAP Two airborne!'

Trevellion's mind was racing. The Harriers should be among the mid-course guidance aircraft within minutes now, but even with their Skyflashes, the Harriers could knock down only eight . . . and the remaining seven Badgers could still guide the Northern Fleet's missiles adequately.

'I agree with you, Pascoe,' Druce murmured behind him. 'Tell 'em to get in among 'em *after* firing their Skyflashes. They've *got* to break up the formation.'

'Order CAP Two to follow up with their cannon,' Trevellion snapped. This is what they enjoyed, what he had revelled in when he had been a fighter pilot in fixed-wing aircraft: there was nothing as exhilarating as a dog-fight, but the Badgers and Bears were well armed against this form of attack.

Gloucester was on the air, her PWO's voice verging on boredom:

'Main raid is now at 074° sixty miles. Mach one decimal two. Losing height from four thousand metres ... one thousand, five ... strength one hundred and fifty.'

Seconds later: 'Firing chaff ... birds fired.'

This was the difficult decision, the vital moment. Enough time must be allowed for the chaff decoy to bloom – yet it must not be distributed too early or the decoy would drift downwind, too far astern.

He switched from *Gloucester*'s loop, listened to his own PWO. The AWO (Air) was doing well, the details of the air picture showing up clearly on the command display.

Then Craddock came up:

'Emergency, sir. 833's got a one-engine failure. She's jettisoning her remaining fuel now. Can you turn into the wind, sir?'

'You're lucky,' Trevellion said. 'I need come up only thirty degrees. Turning now.'

'Roger, sir. I'll try to get her down before CAP One's due in.'

'Officer of the watch; bring her round to starboard to 245°. Yeoman: tell the screen to disregard me.'

'Aye, aye, sir.'

If there was any danger of collision, the officer of the watch could 'over-ride': *Köln* seemed a bit close ...

'Course, sir, 245°.'

The helo that was in trouble must be Gamble's. He ought to be able to get away with it: they'd already be clearing the flight deck for him. He'd be sweeping in, low over the round-down, brakes off, wheels down, flopping in for his running-landing – the squadron had exercised the emergency often enough.

The ops officer cut in:

'UKADGE still can't help us, sir. The RAF's committing maximum effort to the defence of the oil platforms and the east coast.'

So, when the crunch came, the Force was on its own.

'833's safely on, sir.' Craddock came in on the internal link. 'I'm having to use the main lift to strike her down into the hangar. The sea's too bad for the side lift.'

'Well done, Wings,' Trevellion said. 'Get her below before CAP One lands on to re-arm. I'll be needing the Harriers again in a hurry.'

'Time to refuel, sir?'

'No!' Pascoe regretted his impatient retort, even as he shouted it. 'Get them back into the Badgers.' He called to the officer of the watch: 'Bring her back to port to her MLA of 215°.'

Gloucester and the rest of the force were pushing out their ECM. The first Backfires had fired their missiles.

'Main raid: 075° forty,' the PWO (Air) was telling the GDB. '*Gloucester*'s taking them with Sea Darts.' He paused, then continued calmly:

'They're loud and clear on 993. You should have no problem in picking 'em up when they're coming in. They're on the forty-eight-mile range scale.'

'Fire the chaff,' the captain ordered.

To Trevellion, it seemed only seconds before the PWO was calling out:

'Here they come! Just entering the twenty-four-mile range scale.'

'Birds fired, sir!' There was time for the chaff to bloom; the wind was about right.

'Okay,' called the imperturbable chief petty officer in the GDB. 'I've got her.' His unshakeable confidence reassured the men incarcerated in this sombre, steel room.

'Missile's now within twenty miles, sir. Low bogey... air attack! A-arcs open...'

Seconds later the operator was reporting again, calm as a judge: 'Crossing rate's going to be too great for us. Okay, I'm happy with 232-0,' he called, quoting the target identification number of the target. 'I've got track of it. You keep an eye out for the other – she should be coming in.'

The Sea Cats could take only missiles coming towards, Trevellion well knew, but could they prevent this one from hitting *Oileus*?

'We're not able to acquire, sir. It's not a threat to us. There's no way *Köln* can take it either. I'm tracking east.'

Trevellion watched the operators, silent, eyes glued to their

PPIs, the fingertips of their right hands twiddling the white tracking-knobs at the side of their scans. He could hear the Bofors pounding away: the Force was down to point-defence.

'CAP One coming in, sir,' Craddock called. 'Request vertical landing.'

'Affirmative.'

Trevellion had nothing but admiration for these Sea Harriers. He did not have to alter the carrier into the wind, even in this gale . . . he could hear the background roar of their nozzles even from the ops room . . . and then, suddenly, bedlam broke loose in the Force as the first regiment of Backfires came in low, streaking along the horizon at two hundred feet. He never knew how many there were – only that the area defence ships and the point-defence system were overwhelmed. *Gloucester*'s Sea Slugs caught one of them. The bomber in its wake caught the disintegrating débris and plunged, flaming, into the sea. They swept in, over thirty of them, some firing at the Force, the remainder flashing on towards the convoy. But STANAVFOR-LANT was ready and had already fired its chaff.

The air controller was shouting above the tumult: a second regiment was on its way. At the same instant, the PWO announced that the Northern Fleet had fired its surface-to-surface SS-N-12s. The Bears and Badgers were guiding them in, but it was doubtful whether CAP Two could get in among them in time. The running battle off Iceland was still at fever pitch. One of the battle-cruisers, with its attendant force of cruisers and DDGs, was breaking through and dashing towards the convoy. The SS-N-12 attacks were murderous, swamping the ECCM put up by the convoy.

Trevellion listened to the commodore's reports of the devastation the missiles were causing among the ships of his convoy, in spite of the clouds of chaff drifting down-wind above HX–OS I.

'*Low bogey*, zero-four-five, one decimal –'

The ops room was tense while they listened to the GDB, Old Fury's penultimate line of defence. Trevellion held his breath, waiting with the others. The Sea Cats were taking the lone missile and tracking it in. He listened to the clipped reports – and then the anti-missiles were going wide, deceived by the

ECCM of the approaching enemy missile which was skimming at wavetop height above the breaking seas.

Trevellion braced himself, itching to be on his bridge. He tensed for the impact, then, hearing the thumping of the Bofors, their barking penetrating even the steel-reinforced ops room, he jumped up from the command chair. 'I'm going to the bridge,' he growled.

If the missile evaded the steel splinters from the Bofors' barrage, nothing could now save the carrier from a direct hit.

21

HMS Furious, 17 April. Hob Gamble scrambled from the door of his cab, bent double and raced after his crew who were already half-way across the pitching, slippery deck. He ducked as the Sea Cats opened fire from the island. As he ran, he heard the roar from the first of the Sea Harriers returning to rearm. The armourers crouched against the superstructure, waiting to pounce out with the Skyflash missiles.

The handlers were bringing up on the after lift the last of the cabs – any helo which could stay in the sky was good enough now. The men in the coloured jerkins were struggling frenziedly, their trolleys sliding on the greasy deck as the carrier dipped, plunging into the hungry, malevolent seas with which they were learning to live. Hob reached the screen door which Osgood was holding open against the roll. It slammed behind him and, as Hob was reporting the duff port engine, he felt a tap on his shoulder:

'SPLOT,' the duty pilot said. 'Wings wants you in Flyco.'

Slinging his bone dome at Osgood, Hob hurried along the passage and climbed the ladders to the bridge. He pushed out through the final door to the enclosed flat to watch the flight deck, while he regained his breath.

The expanse of wet steel glistened silver-grey in the approaching dusk, where the handlers were wrestling with the Sea King on the main lift which was appearing from beneath deck level. The Bofors were pounding away and he recognized the phumph! of the Sea Cats as the launchers loosed off their second salvo. He saw the spurts of smoke, watched the missiles discharging – this was only the second time he had seen the operation – and then, inexplicably, a blast of air sent him reeling backwards. He splayed his hands to save himself as an orange flash blinded him momentarily. He heard the roar of an explosion, felt the ship shudder. Then another, and another, three in all, at split-second intervals. There was a searing blast of heat, the smell of burning and again that strange, fluttering noise. Dazed, he picked himself from the deck, as Trevellion pushed past him, hurrying to the bridge.

Hob shook his head to clear his reeling senses. He glanced over the lip of the screen abutting the after end of the Flyco projection.

The Flyco bridge was a tangled mass of twisted steel. The projection itself was hanging askew at a crazy angle over the flight deck. The mangled remains of the control centre were burning and from inside the inferno, the groans of trapped men escaped above the crackling flames and the battering of the wind. Hob glanced aft to where the second missile had struck.

Black smoke was beginning to spurt from the hole where the main lift had been. He could see the lift, canted upwards, blown sideways. The helicopter, lying on its side, was burning fiercely, the crimson flames fanned by the wind. The fuel had ignited and the lift area was a sea of fire. The driver of the trolley had been caught underneath his towing trolley. The fire fighters were trying to extract the poor fellow but they were being beaten back by the inferno. Hob turned away, shocked, but then saw more bodies sprawled at the base of the after end of the island.

The third missile must have struck here, for the corner of the island had disappeared to leave an open gash from which pipes, cables and wires now dangled like entrails. He could see the Sea Cat crews, waiting helplessly at their mounting for the re-loads which were failing to come up from below. Those men who remained alive among the flight deck parties were frenziedly trying to cope with Sea King 833 which had been hurled against the island.

The flight deck officer was in the thick of it, goading, leading the shattered team to superhuman efforts. They had to secure the rogue cab before its ten tons crushed everything and everyone in its path as it charged across the rolling deck. Hob was suddenly conscious that the ship had taken on a list, not steep as yet, but approaching ten degrees, perhaps because she was turning at speed? He could see her wake curling away into the dusk. Then, as he tried to gather his thoughts, the main safety valves lifted. The steam roared, a shattering blast, overwhelming everything, forcing the bridge personnel to shout at the top of their voices, their open mouths soundless in their faces...

Hob saw the first of the Sea Harriers streaking in across the port quarter; then two more, the pilots obviously confused by the turn of events. They could not attempt a vertical landing until the fires were extinguished ... They might try to land on one of the convoy's MAC ships – if any such remained – or on *Oileus*' deck. They had come in to rearm.

The officer of the watch was beckoning him from the bridge, his words inaudible. Hob hurried forward, leaning against the list; the safety valves suddenly closed, restoring relative peace, and the officer's words bellowed aft:

'Lieutenant Gamble – Captain.'

'Sir?'

Trevellion stood in the centre of his bridge, calmly conning his ship, his battered pipe, wire-bound and chamfered around the bowl, stuck obstinately into his mouth. He removed it as he tried to telephone the engine-room again.

'MEO?' he asked. 'How's things?'

He leaned against the list, listening to his engineer officer. 'Right, chief. You'll be in the engine-room: the senior's in the damage control centre? Roger.'

As he hung up, the OOW reported:

'NUC lights hoisted, sir.' The two not-under-command lights were casting their red glow upon the bridge area.

'Thanks. Sound two short blasts. *Köln*'s getting too close.'

Hob peered through the windows into the gathering darkness. *Furious* was turning out of control, her rudders jammed hard-over.

'Stop both engines,' Trevellion ordered. 'I'll ease up until the chief can give us power again on the steering engines. He's trying to rig secondary electrical power now. He thinks the main cables have been cut somewhere in the island section, at the after end of the hangar.'

The ops room was coming through again, power restored:

'Ops room – captain. Main computer on the board again – forty-plus bogies on their way.'

'Roger. Go hard-a-starboard, Officer of the Watch.'

They watched the rudder indicators responding and then the ship began to steady up from her crazy circling. The German frigate, *Köln*, was also under full rudder, alive to the danger of collision. She was rearing into the cascading seas, the flying spume a ghostly veil in the darkening twilight. She was heeling heavily to the turn, canting outwards, her turtle-backed upper deck under water as she swung. In the background, the ops room was tracking another regimental attack from some thirty-five Backfires, their target evidently the convoy. Then Hob heard the alarm in the PWO's warning:

'Low bogey coming straight –'

A blinding flash lit up the carrier's port side. A crimson sheet of flame shot upwards from amidships in the German frigate's upper deck.

'My God,' the captain murmured. 'The poor devils.'

Hob was mesmerized by the scene ... *Köln*, like a slow-motion film, was rolling over to her beam-ends. The water boiled white, the seas spouting upwards in furious geysers, the spray drifting downwind and covering her with a shroud of fern-like tracery. The brown anti-fouling of her bottom gleamed momentarily, her two propellers scything in the cauldron as her stern kicked skywards. Then she was gone, driving at full speed into her boiling, watery grave.

'Go below and see what's happening, Gamble,' Trevellion rapped. 'Why's no ammunition getting to the Sea Cats? CAP Two's due back soon. Tell the Chief he's *got* to get the list off her.'

Hob saluted and as he turned he heard Trevellion muttering to himself as he jammed the pipe back into his mouth: 'What are they doing to my beautiful ship?'

As Hob slid down the ladders, the emergency lighting glinting balefully on the polished hand rails. He had so often wondered what action would be like, this blood and guts side of it, in contrast to drowning upside down in his cab. He felt strangely remote from it all, intent only on doing the job in hand, however frightful the horrors. As he reached the Burma Road, he dodged past a couple of men slithering aft against the heavy list, a terribly mutilated man slung between them.

'Where are you taking him?' Hob asked. 'D'you need help?'

'We're okay, sir. Can we get through to the wardroom? The other side's wrecked.'

'I'll come back if I can't get through,' Hob said, hurrying onwards. Then the lights went out. The darkness was absolute. He could hear men cursing behind him and, as he groped for the fore-and-aft bulkheads on the outboard side of the passageway, he guessed that he must have reached the for'd end of the hangar section. It was getting hot down here. At the far end of the tunnel he could see the flickering of flames...

Without warning, he fell suddenly into a void beneath his feet... He was winded when he came up all-standing, his hands torn by the jagged metal which had caught him, but which had prevented him from falling headlong to the deck below. As he hauled himself upwards, the lights came on, flickered, went out again: another few feet and he would have been flung to the galley stoves below, where they were trying to sort out the chaos. He regained the passageway and began stumbling aft, when the lights snicked on again. At the corner of the flat, the first lieutenant and a sick berth tiffy were crouching over a man whose guts spilled upon the corticene.

'I've given him too much morphia, a double dose.' The officer's face was white, his eyes angry. 'Tell the PMO, Gamble. Ask him what I can do.'

Hob rushed on towards where the hatchway to the damage control headqarters should be. The heat was becoming unbearable, the plating hot beneath his shoes. He could go no further, halted by a group of men working frenziedly in the passage. The master-at-arms was in charge, his clipped orders spurring the damage control party. He tossed a crowbar to a burly seaman.

'Get stuck in, Roper,' he panted.

Hob waited impatiently to shove his way past them. The ship was rolling unnaturally, jerking the men off their balance as they tried to enlarge the hole which they had ripped open in the bulkhead.

'The main drain's blocked in the hangar,' the master shouted at him. 'They've flooded the hangar and the water can't get away. There's hundreds of tons of free-flood in there.'

They took it in turns tearing, wrenching and levering at the widening gash. As the mass of water slopped to starboard, jets of water spurted into the passageway. 'I can't get the oxygen burners, sir,' the master yelled. 'Look out when this stuff clears!' He shoved a couple of men from the route to clear the passageway. On the far side, Hob stumbled into the chief gunnery instructor. 'What's up?' Hob asked. The man's face was grey, dripping with sweat and he seemed all-in.

'Magazine's about to go up,' he gasped. 'There's men in there, sir, and we can't get 'em out. Impossible to supply missiles to the mountings – can't get near 'em in this heat. We've got to flood, sir. I can't get through to the bridge,' he gasped. 'Communication's gone.'

'I'll report to the captain, chief,' Hob shouted. 'Get back to the magazine: I'll find you there.'

The chief nodded, then stumbled back towards the smoke and steam whence he had emerged. Hob rushed for'd again, past the master's party of stalwarts, as a river of sea water began deluging down the passageway.

He fell again in the passageway of the deck above, where they were laying out the dead and wounded on the slippery, blood-soaked deck. He tried to ignore the groans, to blot out the carnage. He stumbled past the dying and through the damage control parties who were stoically trying to restore power by running the emergency electrical cables. When finally he reached the door of the ops room, he stumbled inside, trying to recover his breathing. The admiral was crouched over the command display.

'Rosy's hitting 'em,' Druce said. 'I've got him loud and clear.' The dark eyes gleamed as he glanced round at his officers. 'Where's the captain?'

'On the bridge, sir,' soo said.

'Get him – with my compliments,' Druce snapped. 'STRIG-RUTWO's hit the control battle-cruiser, smack in the vitals.'

'Aye, aye, sir.'

'UKADGE says the Tornados will be with them at any minute, sir.' There was an edge to the PWO's voice. 'They're co-ordinating with COMAAFCE's FI5s. The fighters are going straight in.'

'Roger.' Druce glanced round for his flag-lieutenant.

'Satellite above the horizon yet, flags?'

'Any moment, sir.'

'Get out my sitrep. Don't include the convoy casualties until after it has completed its turn.'

The PWO (Air) cut in:

'Another Backfire attack on the way, sir. Regimental strength.'

Druce nodded.

'Is CAP Two on its way back yet?'

'Yes, sir – but one Harrier only. They got nine Badgers.'

Druce rubbed his bristly chin. He said softly in the silence, 'It'll be interesting, gentlemen, to see if the enemy can keep up his co-ordinated attacks, now Rosy's got at his heart.'

The ops room crew concentrated in there, fighting the battle, seemed oblivious that Old Fury might be blowing up sky-high at any moment. Hob parted the curtains and hurried to the darkness of the bridge. Trevellion was silhouetted against the indigo windows. He was sucking at his pipe and peering into the darkness.

'Captain, sir.'

'Ah, Gamble.' He faced Hob, the grey eyes steady.

'The list's caused by free-flood water in the hangar, sir: they're draining down now. I couldn't get to the damage control HQ. The magazine area's on fire, sir. The Sea Cat and torpedo magazines are hotting up. They're requesting permission to flood. It's vital for the safety of the ship, they say . . .' He added softly: 'The magazine crews are inside, sir. They can't get 'em out.'

Trevellion turned away, staring again into the night. The enemy air attacks had not let up for over an hour: the attack of the second regiment of Backfires had been murderous, swamping the Force's and the convoy escorts' ECM. No reliable casualty report had yet come in. The convoy had been caught half-way through the turn, but the majority, it appeared, had steadied on their new course for Fair Isle. The third attack had been the bloodiest, synchronized with fresh attacks from the surviving SSNs. The Backfires had come in thick and fast: the low-fliers had closed much sooner than expected, once the defences had been swamped. No one, not even Druce, had dared to ask what effect the slaughter had upon the escorts and STANAVFORLANT. Oslo was a world away yet.

As Hob waited in the darkness, he could hear the hissing of the oxygen burners on the port side of the bridge, where they were cutting away the steel to free the trapped Flyco team. He glanced at the officer of the watch, his eyes posing the inquiry.

'They've got Little F out,' was the answer. 'But the others . . .' and he shook his head. 'They had to cut Wings out.' The officer turned away, jamming the binoculars to his eyes, searching for the ships of the screen.

'Gamble?' Trevellion snapped from the window.

'Sir?'

'I can't fight the ship without the Sea Cats. Get down there again. Tell 'em to put the bloody fire out.'

22

HMS Furious, 18 April. The night seemed the longest which Captain Trevellion had ever known; this was certainly to be one of the longest days.

'I'll be in the wings of the bridge,' he told them in the fusty ops room.

Out here, watching the silver-streaked dawn imperceptibly emerging, with its layers of olive-green and rose-tipped clouds, he could hope to recover some of his inner tranquillity. *Furious* was still afloat, but the price was cruelly high: in addition to the battle casualties, nine of the missile room's crew had been drowned. Trevellion's thankfulness that his ship was still able to fight was marred by the remorse and the gnawing doubt he felt for the terrible decision he had been forced to take when he had deliberately ordered the flooding of the magazines. The sacrifice of those nine men had saved the ship and, consequently, the convoy was still forging ahead, albeit at only twelve knots.

Pascoe Trevellion stared aft, to the dark horizon where the night clouds still rolled in unending succession towards the Arctic wastes. A loaded calm had descended upon the opposing forces, but the gulls had returned, wheeling and screaming in the old ship's wake.

Trevellion had snatched no sleep for forty-one hours. He had long since passed the weariness which craved slumber: he had reached that limbo where he reacted to events only because he had been endlessly drilled and trained for so many years: he was reacting like an automaton, numbed, insensitive to the professional decisions he had to make. As he gazed aft, stifling his yawn, he could see the cross-trees of *Athabaskan*'s mast tipping the horizon.

Furious was twenty miles ahead of the remains of the convoy which was now settled down on its new course of 108°. The commodore, who had survived destruction in spite of being selected by the Backfires as the prime target, had reported the sickening news of nine ships sunk and that only eight ships of HX–OS1 still survived. One of the casualties, a troopship, had not been seen again after the second Backfire attack. Over five thousand men must have perished during the dark and terrible night.

The remainder were battling on, though one more had been sunk when at 0300 the convoy had passed through the enemy SSK line R, consisting of four diesel boats between Sule Skerry and Foula. The Sea Kings, now out of torpedoes because of the fire in the magazines and because of their continuous counter-attacks, were continuing their Jez runs and vectoring STANAV-FORLANT's ships on to the targets. All four SSKs had been sunk, one rammed by *Jesse L. Brown*, who was now limping back through the Minches to the Clyde, her bows stove in. *Penelope*'s Ikara had accounted for a second; *Goeben*'s Lynx for another; and *Athabaskan*'s Sea Kings for the last. *Tidespring*, their re-plenishment ship, had been hit but was managing to keep up.

Trevellion stood capless, allowing the breeze to blow through his thinning hair. It was good to be here, at last in relatively sheltered waters and in better weather conditions, now that the interminable gales were moderating – force seven and still easing, which was giving the frigates a welcome let-up. How they had battled on, day after day, night after night, and still been able to fight their ships at the crucial moment, was a measure of their efficiency and of the resolution and stamina of the men who served in them . . . and out here, alone on the wings of his bridge, Trevellion felt uplifted. They had reached Fair Isle, but Oslo was still a long way off: thirty-two hours, if the enemy carried out no further attacks.

There had been that moment of private despair last night when he was convinced that the Battle of Bill Bailey's Bank was about to be classed with PQ 17, the worst convoy disaster of all time. When the fourth regimental Backfire attack was sweeping in, he had known that nothing could save the convoy. That was also the instant when Rosy Boyd's Flash Report came through, when STRIGRUTWO began mixing it with the enemy. At 1926, three of Rosy's strike aircraft hit one of the battle-cruisers (she

158

must have been the command ship) at the instant when our ECCM began to take real effect.

The battle-cruiser had hauled from the action, her bridge and midship section crippled: it could have been no coincidence that this was the moment when the co-ordination of the enemy's air attacks began disintegrating. The Tornados from UKADGE turned up at the critical instant too, followed by a superbly timed strike by COMAAFCE'S FI5S: they shot the Forgers from the sky, before hitting the enemy surface ships with their missiles.

Rosy Boyd's boys finished off the remainder: the other battle-cruiser, who also had turned to intercept the convoy, retired at full speed. Rosy had ordered 'general chase', but the severely mauled Northern Fleet had reversed its course at speed, beneath the horde of Soviet aircraft sent out to shield them, to become lost in the Arctic seas. Rosy was racing south and would be entering the North Sea tonight, to cover the arrival of the three trans-Atlantic convoys which were expected at their arrival ports on the 20, 21 and 22 April: Oslo, Le Havre and Rotterdam.

One of the worst moments for Trevellion had been when, in the midst of last night's battle, the second Sea Harrier CAP had been unable to land-on, because of the fire and the worsening list. The aircraft had run out of fuel and had ditched alongside the ships of the screen. All the aircraft had been lost and their pilots with them, for the seas were impossible and the temperatures barely above freezing. Those gallant men had given their lives but, by breaking up the guidance Bears and Badgers, they had prevented the Backfires from annihilating the convoy.

And his own Sea King squadron? The survivors, only seven of them now, were out on their feet with exhaustion. Little F was managing to keep going from a jury Flyco rigged abaft the bridge. Wing's body, with the other seventy-three dead, was lined on the quarterdeck, waiting for burial when there was time. The air engineer officer and his magnificent team were managing to keep six helos in the air; three crews were resting, while the seventh cab was being maintained as the stop-gap. The remnants of the squadron were trying to maintain a modified ASW screen seventy miles ahead: at this moment they were in contact with the Lima line of seven SSKS which the LRMP aircraft had confirmed. *Furious'* Sea Kings (all three of them) were holding them down, pinging away, while they waited for help . . .

Flag Officer First Flotilla was on his way back, thank God. At 0400 this morning, he had responded immediately to Druce's call for help. Leaving the Nimrod and a frigate to keep down the heads of the SSKS north-east of Muckle Flugga off the Shetlands, Flag Officer First Flotilla, flying his flag in the damaged *Illustrious*, was steaming directly to line Lima to relieve our Sea Kings. The ASW cruiser with its protective umbrella of Sea Harriers and its fresh squadron of helicopters was what Force Q needed at this moment.

The Force had suffered: *Köln* sunk; *Brazen*, struck by three direct hits from AS-6 missiles, had burnt out and sunk in the raging gale. No one could help her: 260 of her company had perished. Only *Gloucester* remained and her one Sea Dart mounting was useless through lack of ammunition. If *Phoebe* failed to rejoin with *Ungava Bay*, Force Q was defenceless from air attack. The sooner Flag Officer First Flotilla arrived with his two air defence ships, the better . . . The latest ASW cruiser, *Ark Royal*, was in the North Sea covering the rigs; *Invincible* was refitting, long overdue through strikes – she could have been useful just now.

Trevellion wondered what the final score between Rosy Boyd and Stukalov had been: Boyd's place was down here now, to combat any further air strikes when the convoys neared the bottle-necks at the entrance to the ports. The best thing that had happened so far was the mining, first of the Kattegat by the Danes, then of the Skagerrak by the Norwegians and their Danish Nato partners: a sortie by the Soviet Baltic Fleet from Baltiysk, or by enemy submarines from Liepaja would be embarrassing at the moment. Attacks by the Naval Air Force from Kaliningrad were a certainty.

'Mug o' soup, sir?'

Trevellion turned. His steward, Blair, dressed in his white tunic and clean-shaved even after helping the PMO all night with the wounded in the wardroom, held the steaming mug towards him.

160

Blair remained until the tomato soup was drained.

'Message from the admiral, sir. He's happy to take over, if you'd like to get your head down.'

A grin twitched in Trevellion's face. Roderick Druce obviously itched to command a ship again.

'Thank him, Blair.' He handed back the empty mug. 'But tell the Officer of the Watch to shake me at the first sign of anything.'

23

Sea King 826, 19 April. Aircrewman Thomas Osgood banged the side of his bone dome with his fist. His eyelids continued to droop, the effort of keeping awake literally a physical pain. The vibration and the racket of 826 made him sleepier, rather than keeping him awake – and in the darkness at the back of the aircraft he tried to read his wrist watch: 0229. His tired brain was sluggish: twilight began at 0352 (he had written it down on his knee-pad during the briefing). He glanced slyly down, half-smiling to himself. He was incapable of thought, was going round the twist – yes, there it was: twilight 0352, one hour thirteen minutes before that streak of first light should begin to show. Charlie-time was 0630: four hours before he could get in some zeds again.

It seemed only a flick of time since their last sortie, though the remaining Sea Kings weren't much use now: but, even without torpedoes, by going active with 195, at least the helos were forcing the ssks to keep their heads down. It had been a massacre when finally Flag Officer First Flotilla had turned up yesterday afternoon, during Osgood's last sortie but one – of the seven enemy diesel boats reckoned to be in line Lima, Flag Officer First Flotilla and *Illustrious'* Sea Kings claimed four. After clearing the area, one of our new diesel boats had sunk another.

'You okay, Oz?' Dunker was asking. 'Ball ready?'

'Yes, sir. All set.'

'We'll do a modified when we get there,' Dunker called to the pilots. 'Ten minutes and we'll be there. Active only: won't be needing the buoys.'

Lieutenant Gamble's voice sounded as worn as anyone's when he acknowledged the observer's instructions. With a duff engine, the running-landing in the thick of the battle had not been easy: he had dealt with the emergency with ice-cool precision, like an exercise at Culdrose.

At last, they were approaching the last of the suspected enemy submarine lines blocking the convoy's route into the Skagerrak: twelve diesel boats, spread across a circle with its centre 180 miles due west of the Skaw, were reputed to be in the area. The remaining helos of 814 had to keep the enemy down with 195 until Flag Officer First Flotilla, belting up from astern, could deal with them.

Phoebe had rejoined: Old Fury needed her as point-defence ship. The convoy had taken *Ungava Bay* under its wing, for she was able to keep up the twelve knots: with her precious cargo, she was shepherded bang into the middle of the flock. She'd done well, slipping through the Pentland Firth.

Osgood sensed the tension in Dunker's crouching silhouette in front of him; the observer was peering intently at his radar screen and checking his doppler navigator. Nothing seemed real now to Osgood. He was so exhausted that, when told by the master-at-arms that he would be court-martialled for suspected murder when they got home, he had merely shaken his head. He hadn't seen Kotta for days: the PO was keeping well clear – he might even be among the corpses on the quarterdeck – a pity, that, because his death would make Osgood's defence much trickier. And Gwen? He prayed often for her safety now, in the dark loneliness at the back of the cab: there was nothing more he could do. Dunker was straightening his back:

'Hob, I've got two groups of echoes on my screen: twenty-nine miles, zero-five-five: one formation is just separating from the other, both on the same bearing.'

'Get a Flash to Mother,' Gamble ordered. 'Breaking silence can't hurt now.'

Captain Trevellion and the ASW group commander had been watching the fast attack craft attack developing ever since the Norwegian Neptune's first sighting and 826's report at 0246. The Norwegians had come up also, stating that their own FACs, eight *Hauks*, had attacked from ten miles with their Penguin missiles and were returning to Haakonsvern to rearm. Results weren't known, but two of the enemy, presumed to be Osa IIs, were thought to have blown up. The radar echoes had not faded

163

and were still on a steady bearing of 028°, range thirty-one miles and closing.

The captain looked at the ops room clock: 0355. Dawn must be on its way; the Soviets had judged things well.

'They must have come from Narvik,' Druce said. 'They've got a range of only eight hundred miles at cruising speed.'

'They're lucky with the weather, sir,' Trevellion said. 'This fog's in their favour. They'll be refuelling at sea.'

'Stand-by Sea Cats,' the PWO (Air) rapped. 'Take the Styx at one decimal five.'

'They'll open fire at maximum range,' Druce said. 'They don't know we've only one mounting.'

'Thank God *Gloucester* could ammunition from *Oileus*, sir,' Trevellion said. 'The destroyer's well on the up-side.'

'*Phoebe*'s well placed too – and she has the advantage of seventy-five per cent ammunition remaining.'

Their dubious sense of security did not last long. The fighter controller was chipping in: 'Forty-plus bogies taking off, range one-twenty, coming in from the east, sir. Buda gives another regiment rounding North Cape: Backfires.'

They watched the co-ordinated attacks. *Illustrious* was scrambling her Sea Harriers, all five of them. Even if they met them head-on and reached the scene in time (at height, the Backfires were doing Mach 2.5) the Harriers could not cope with the numbers. But where were the Bears and Badgers? Satellite mid-course guidance, possibly? Hopefully this fog might make things more difficult, and our ECM might be more effective this time.

'Stand-by chaff,' Trevellion ordered. 'It's a pity the RAF's so engaged elsewhere.'

'Being your Group Commander,' Roderick Druce said, the lights flickering in his dark eyes, 'I must point out that we have one great advantage: Flag Officer First Flotilla is between the Backfires and the convoy. I presume that we're the prime target.'

Trevellion found it difficult to grin back: Old Fury must always be high on the high value target table.

'CINCEASTLANT confirms maximum jamming, sir.'

'Very good,' Trevellion acknowledged. ECM from ashore, at

sea and from the satellites were our best hope against these swamping tactics.

'*Gloucester*'s engaging, sir. She's fired her birds.'

Trevellion nodded. He touched the command computer buttons.

'Range of the Osas?' he snapped. 'Could *Phoebe* take them with her Exocets?'

'Twenty miles, sir.'

Another three miles and *Phoebe* would be within range. Surely the Osas wouldn't make that mistake...?

'FACS opening fire. Stand-by Sea Cats,' the PWO (Surface) called. 'Alter course to 020° to open A arcs, sir.'

'Bring her round, officer of the watch,' Trevellion ordered over the intercom, 'Course 020°.'

What defence could one Sea Cat mounting put up against the coming rain of missiles from the Osas and Backfires? Even if the after Sea Cat had not been knocked out in the convoy battle, the carrier's own defence could not begin to cope.

'*Phoebe* engaging with Exocets, sir.'

The Backfires would be launching at any second. He watched them, fascinated, crawling across the air display, while the PWO (Air) tracked them in.

'Low bogies, sir. 020° and 070°. Range, one seven.'

And then he listened to *Gloucester* being overwhelmed while attempting to reload ... 'She's on fire and sinking, sir. They're abandoning ship.'

The missiles were streaking towards Old Fury. Trevellion watched them until the Sea Slug began to take them.

'I'm going on the bridge, sir,' he called to Druce. 'I can do nothing more here.'

He sprang from his chair and rushed out to the port wing, yelling at the officer of the watch to relay his orders: he could try to con his ship away from the murderous missiles. He glimpsed one, winging in from the starboard bow. '*Hard-a-starboard!*'

He'd meet it head on, give the Sea Cats and the Bofors their only chance ... He watched the yellow and crimson flames streaking nearer and nearer through the fog, heard the Bofors banging away, smelt the fumes from the Sea Cats. Then the missiles were exploding in mid-air, disintegrating with a sharp crack! He could even see the bits flying, the blast imprinting a fern-like pattern on the calm sea.

It was so still out here, when the guns and the Sea Cats were silent — just the soughing of the breeze as the old carrier ploughed on through the glassy calm, the fog a dirty brown against the moon.

'Alarm starboard, sir!' the lookout was yelling across the bridge from the open door.

Trevellion had no time for a bearing: the thing exploded, shattering the bridge windows and slicing the lookout in half. The captain staggered back into the bridge and took over the con himself:

'Tell me where they're coming from!'

But it was no use. Again and again, he felt that sickening thud, the shuddering of her hull as the missiles struck. A fire was raging abaft the bridge; the Sea Cat had ceased firing, but the Bofors were still barking defiantly. There was a flash and a strange fluttering sound . . . then the bridge exploded in his face and an excruciating pain stabbed in his right thigh.

In Sea King 826 they had been listening to the battle from the moment the Norwegian FACs broke away. They cheered when the Lynxs from STANAVFORLANT and Flag Officer First Flotilla had got in among the Osas after the surface action. Their Sea Skuas had wreaked fair old vengeance – at least four of the FACs were burning wrecks and two would never reach Narvik. But the exuberance ceased when they listened to *Goeben*'s Lynx falling in flames into the sea. They flew back to Mother in silence, after the attack on *Illustrious* by the Backfires which had sheered off from *Furious*. They had streaked straight for the ASW cruiser and sunk her, a blazing wreck, while her Harriers were still clawing after the second wave of Backfires.

And then, from fifteen hundred feet, Hob spotted Old Fury, the grand old ship who had fought so hard. He saw the smoke first, trailing to leeward in the breeze which had got up with the dawn to waft away the fog. She lay stopped, on fire from stem to stern, *Phoebe* standing guard and tearing around under continuous rudder.

'Charlie-time again?' Hob demanded.

'0640 – and that's the latest possible,' Dunker replied. The clock on the panel showed 0628.

'We'll have to risk it – or ditch,' Hob said. 'All ready in the back? Harnesses all round?'

'Checked!' Grog said, glancing at Hob.

'Yeah,' Dunder called. 'Ozzie's strapping in.'

In silence Hob took the cab down, to take a closer look at the flight deck. The HCO was still in contact, taking him down calmly, vectoring him for a ship control approach: no fire danger right aft, he had commented, between the round-down and the wrecked lift. The other two cabs of the sortie were to follow 826 in ...

'God,' Grog murmured, 'look at her list, Hob.'

Hob had said nothing. *Furious* was down by the bows and listing heavily to port.

'When we get down, we could slip over the side,' Hob said. 'I'll try to hold her until they've got the lashings on.'

The HCO was ordering them on to spot 8.

'She's a sitting duck,' Grog said. 'It only needs the Backfires to come back.'

'Another regiment,' Hob said. He was nudging her gently towards the round down when Grog shouted:

'*Fighters*, Hob! Over to the left, low.'

Hob dared not take his eyes off the line.

'They're Norwegian,' Grog cried. 'The Scowegians are here!'

'Good news,' Hob said softly as the flight deck came up towards him, canted at a hideous angle. 'They'll be from Søla, near Stavanger. The old lady'll be all right after all.'

But his words sounded false. They all knew the chances were bleak. ETA Oslo was 2300 tonight – a long way yet. The convoy (or what was left of it) was just below the horizon, depending for its only defence on the crippled carrier and her remaining escort. A long, long day lay ahead before they could safely pass through the gate of the controlled minefield off the Skaw.

A thousand yards to go ... he could see the handlers crouching in the nets waiting to spring out as the cab touched ... bloody lucky she wasn't rolling. Then he saw the yawning gash clipping the perimeter of spot 8, from which belched spurts of dirty, yellow-tinged smoke.

24

HMS Furious, 19 April. The captain of HMS *Furious* stood alone on the signal bridge above his wheelhouse. He had slept for three hours after passing Farsund, the first sighting of Norway for which they had craved for so long. Was it really only a week since he had taken the carrier out of Mount's Bay? A lifetime had been crammed into these seven days.

A shave followed by high tea with Druce in his bridge cabin, and Trevellion felt more like himself, in spite of the wound in his right leg. They'd taken him down to the sick bay, but he had come round almost at once, during the precarious descent down the ladders. He had a deep gash, mercifully missing the artery, and poor old John Bellairs now seemed disappointed at not being able to stay on the bridge as second-in-command.

And here was his ship, seven miles from the 'gate' into the controlled minefield between Denmark and Norway which had sealed the Baltic, with the exception, perhaps, of a limited number of intrepid enemy submarines: the pleasant signal from the Commander Allied Forces Baltic Approaches was good to get. *Furious* had been saved from further air attacks by the Norwegian Air Force fighters from Søla: they had given him precious time to get his ship under way again. It had been an emotional moment, too, watching the Norwegian frigates from Haakonsvern steaming at full speed to the westward to help bring in the convoy during this last and potentially hazardous phase. Lurking submarines and predatory aircraft always hung about the nodal points.

The port authorities in Oslo were ready for the convoy. Intensive night mining from enemy aircraft had been suspected (the major north European ports had all suffered intensely): and the swept-channel had yielded over 280 enemy mines of the most intricate sort. The last sweep into the Oslo approaches had been completed less than an hour ago, though, with these most modern beasts, a 'negative' sweep was no recipe for immunity.

There they were ... and Trevellion squinted towards the pale sun which hung over the western horizon to where the convoy, the commodore proudly in the van, was approaching in single file from below the horizon. Trevellion nodded to the officer of the watch who was out in the wings on the deck below:

'Clear lower deck. Bring her round to the reciprocal.'

Cleaning into number eights would do the troops a lot of good, after these appalling days. Watching the merchantmen steam past would remind them all that, if our lot had been unpleasant, those brave men in their defenceless ships had endured much worse. Morale had not been helped by the stench of death 'tween decks. Many bodies could not be extricated from the tangled steel where the missiles had gouged out the ship's guts. The ship would need dockyard assistance before the appalling remains could finally be removed. All the remedial measures the PMO and the commander had tried could not disguise the smell of putrefaction; near the flats and passageways, canvas screens had helped to hide the worst of the horrendous evidence of death.

The carrier was swinging now, settling to her homeward course for the Straits of Dover and for Plymouth; he would keep her at twelve knots until past the convoy. He watched the first of his ship's company trickling through the screen doors to take up their positions on the edge of the flight deck.

The evening was hazy – more fog in the offing? He could see the low-lying foreshore, a grey-green line on the northern horizon. He had glimpsed, just after Farsun, the smudge of white-capped mountains far away, to the east of Stavanger. It was futile to remind himself that, eight hundred miles to the north, the invader was still ensconced and had yet to be thrown out: when would Britain begin to realize that victory in this frightful struggle was synonymous with survival? The Russians had but to move one kilometre westwards on the central plain and the nuclear exchange would flare.

Survival? The fact that Old Fury had continued to shield the convoy and to remain afloat herself was a miracle and due largely to Trevellion's splendid MEO, a massive, taciturn

Welshman. By his leadership, the chief had inspired his damage control teams to efforts which they themselves had never believed possible: by all logical calculations *Furious* should have sunk, but they had saved her.

The carrier, during the last attack in the early hours this morning, had been hit by seven missiles, two being 'plungers' with near-vertical trajectories. Eventually the DC parties had succeeded in smothering the fires, and then they dealt with the two holes on her port bow, the largest, fifty feet before the bridge, a huge hole just above the water-line. An oil tank had been contaminated and she had taken on a bad list.

The chief had compensated and brought her back to an even keel but it had been a near thing. The compartments were evacuated and the DC parties had rigged up jury collision mats. By keeping the pumps going, the chief had things under control. The chopper pilots had insisted on maintaining their limited screen right up to the minefield ... already, Little F was preparing the next sortie, though there was little room for them now that the after end of the flight deck had become a park for *Illustrious*' Sea Harriers.

Geoffrey Manning, the rear-admiral flying his flag in the ASW cruiser had been an old friend. He had gone down with the rest of them when the Backfires blasted her with everything they had ... when her four remaining Sea Harriers returned to find their deck gone, *Furious*' fighter controller had brought them in one by one to the after spot on the old carrier's deck. The handlers had never moved so fast. Trevellion had never felt more proud of his ship's company.

What a moving sight was the commodore's ship! Bunting was flying from her starboard yardarm – and Pascoe could see the officer who had held this precious convoy together. Tall and bowed, saluting in the wings as his ship slid past the carrier, the older man waved when he heard the cheers from Old Fury's company. They cheered him, again and again, the echoes rebounding as the two ships passed each other at less than two cables. Rusty the length of her, a corner of the bridge gone, her house flag fluttering proudly, the fly in tatters from the gales, she proudly led her six survivors towards the 'gate' through the controlled minefield.

Two more warriors: one, a big liner, her rails lined with cheering Canadian troops, her peacetime finery red with rust. They had begun to camouflage her in Halifax but had completed only half one side; and the other ship, a cargo vessel, her hatches covered with jeeps, over which the tattered remains of flapping tarpaulins threshed in the ship's own wind. She had run up a clean new ensign, the maple leaf flapping defiantly at her stern.

Ungava Bay followed next, precisely in station, but steaming crabwise from the list which she had borne since the opening phase of the battle. The ugly, functional lines of the big container ship emphasized the shambles which had been her upper deck, where the bent Samson posts leaned like windswept poplars. Her paint had gone from the bridge structure aft and the bare steel was charred and stained with rust, like blood. Her siren tooted joyfully as she passed.

Two more damaged ships followed, each listing, the fifth badly down by the bows, the sixth, half a mile astern and trying to keep up. Two huge gashes showed in her side, the edges of her wounds also blackened by the heat from the explosions: she was the other surviving container ship whose poop deck had been converted into a pad for her Sea Harriers – Trevellion could see the remains of one which must have received the blast from the missile explosion abaft the bridge. They had not cleared away the bits and pieces yet, and he could see why: on the after part, just below her ensign, were her dead, lined neatly in rows and covered by bunting, a Canadian flag across the centre – she must be steaming with a skeleton crew. *Furious* remained silent ... and then they cheered the Canadian until they could see only her transom.

'Signal from the commodore, sir,' the yeoman called from his clattering lamp on the signal bridge: 'To ASW Group Commander, *Furious*, *Phoebe* from Commodore HX–OS 1. Message reads: "If you can take it, we can. Keep up the good work of giving the swine a bloody nose. Good luck and a swift recovery. We hope to see you soon to take care of us again."'

Trevellion nodded. The admiral had prepared his farewell and the yeoman was already flashing it across the water:

'Very many thanks. We shall be back soon. Good hunting

to the Canadian Division. Give Ivan the same medicine ashore.'

The blinking light from the wings of the commodore's bridge ceased. The churning screws left their fading wakes astern and *Furious* closed the waiting ships of COMSTANAVFORLANT. They had turned and as the wounded carrier steamed past them, her sides still manned, the bosun's calls shrilled across the still water. It was an emotional moment, as Old Chough stood there alone, returning the salutes of the ships. He watched them, their men cheering, their tattered battle ensigns flying proudly, the blue flag of Nato flapping from their foremasts, battle-proved for the first time. It was a moment he wouldn't forget.

'Is it worth it?' he asked himself, alone on his bridge. The slaughter had been appalling for both sides. Twelve ships had been lost out of a convoy of eighteen: two vast VLCCs; two store ships; two liners crammed with troops, though some may have been picked up by the rescue ships from the US coastguard which had been detailed to bring up the rear; three general-cargo ships; one supply ship and two vehicle carriers, not counting *Ungava Bay* who still carried half her cargo. The convoy escorts had lost one fleet nuclear submarine (a serious blow to the submariners); two frigates and one guided missile destroyer.

Force Q had been hard hit: *Gloucester* overwhelmed, the target for a regiment of Backfires; *Brazen* sunk; *Köln* rolled over and sunk; and *Oileus* damaged in the last Osa attack – a savage, costly battle, but STANAVFORLANT had come out of it miraculously – and Trevellion was certain there was a lesson in that. The other casualties were *Jesse L. Brown* who finally sank after her ramming, *Athabaskan* damaged by a prematurely exploding missile, and *Tidespring*, the replenishment ship, eventually burnt out while being towed to Sollum Voe.

And the helicopters? Only five of the squadron remained, the crews of the Sea King casualties all lost. Anvil had accounted for over half of the losses. The Sea Harriers had proved their worth, but at frightful cost – ninety per cent had failed to return but they had prevented annihilation of the convoy and its covering forces.

And the enemy? From the provisional casualty figure it was

obvious that the enemy had suffered even worse, particularly underwater. Total enemy losses to date were estimated at 158, and Nato's at 52. It had been conclusively demonstrated that if submarines disclosed their presence by carrying out an attack, they would suffer certain destruction. It was difficult to sort out how many kills were due to the covering forces of the HX-OS 1 convoy because the total picture was not yet in. Trevellion extracted the typed sheet from his reefer pocket; it made ugly reading on this soft evening.

Trevellion turned as his navigating officer came up behind him:

'Course set for the Falls light vessel, sir. Speed eighteen knots. Carrying out zigzag number eight.'

'Very good, Pilot. I'll be in the ops room having a look at the world-wide scoreboard. Keep an eye on STANAVFORLANT for me. When do we expect the next submarine threat?'

'Any time from 0400 onwards, sir.'

In the ops room, Druce was waiting for him. SOO had rigged up a blackboard and chalked in the shape of the oceans. He had hung on the bulkhead a large sheet of paper on which he had scrawled the provisional casualties as they had come in from ACLANT. The lights dimmed as SOO first dealt with the Mediterranean, his finger on the Straits of Gibraltar.

The total worked out at five to one in the Allies' favour but we had lost two CVS and a CAH. Nineteen Nato submarines had failed to return.

'And the convoys?' Trevellion asked. 'How have the rest of 'em fared?'

'We've lost sixty-one per cent of the convoy in our HX,' SOO said. 'The other Atlantic convoys, so far, including mining casualties at the ports of arrival, are averaging forty-nine per cent losses.'

The silence was total as SOO listed the appalling casualties, but SACLANT had emphasized: 'We've *got* to get to Europe. We're going to have to *roll over 'em* to get there.' He had not been far wrong.

'Submarines?' Druce asked. 'What's the world casualty figure?'

Trevellion watched as SOO totted up the score – the free

173

world's survival depended on the swift destruction of the enemy's submarine fleet.

'So far ...' SOO drawled, 'SSNS and SSKS ...'

'Are you including SSBNS?' Druce asked.

'No, sir. They've not been involved so far, thank God.'

'So?'

'223 enemy submarines confirmed killed, sir, – world-wide. No confrontation in the Pacific, but the Indian Ocean figures include the Malacca Straits.'

The destruction of the enemy's submarine fleet was even more devastating than the most optimistic forecast before the hostilities began.

'Thanks, SOO,' Roderick Druce said. 'I've heard from the Port Admiral, Devonport: he's ready for us.'

'The funeral service will be at 0930, tomorrow morning, sir,' Trevellion announced quietly before everyone dispersed. 'Matthew would like to start early.'

Druce nodded. 'You'd better get your head down, Pascoe,' he said. 'It's a long way to Guz yet.' They stood up as he left the ops room. After checking the long range plot, Trevellion returned to his bridge. He checked the course, noted that the chief was still managing revolutions for eighteen knots. He wrote up his night order book, then went out into the darkness.

It was chilly in the wings. The mangled wreck of Flyco provided an unpleasant, skeletal effect against the subdued, violet lighting of the flight deck where the final Sea King sortie was warming up. On the carrier's port bow Trevellion could make out the red lights from one of the oil platforms: a lonely, perilous job, under these wartime conditions. The Russian airmen could zap them, one by one, if their masters dared risking escalation.

Furious was ploughing through the night, a darkened ghost-ship, still viable, still able to seek out and sink enemy submarines. It was 450 miles to the Falls, where CINCCHAN's mine-sweepers were waiting. ETA Plymouth Sound was 0900 on Monday morning, 21 April – and Trevellion sighed, alone in his anxiety. A day and a half to survive before they were safe – two enemy submarine areas to negotiate, the first of them in six hours' time. The squadron's five remaining Sea Kings and

STANAFORLANT's whirly-birds would soon be flushing them out...

He pulled out his pipe and began filling it, the wind blowing in his face. He shivered, uneasy. There was more to come, of that he could be sure. His instinct rarely let him down these days. He turned and went inside.

Tomorrow, though it was Sunday, he would try to deal with so much that was outstanding: the personal problems of his men; the reports; the letters to the next of kin; and that deplorable case of suspected murder which was brewing. During a lull in the action, John Bellairs had reported quietly that Petty Officer Kotta had been cut in half by an exploding missile. With Kotta's death, the strain on Osgood must be considerable. Trevellion turned and stepped back into his bridge.

He'd have a smoke in his cabin before hitting his sack. In thirty-six hours, he might be talking to Rowena – but he thrust the thought from his mind, as superstitious as most Cornishmen. He shivered again, but not from the cold. His instinct and his training were warning him that he mustn't let up, nor allow his company to relax for an instant. Old Fury was a thorn in the enemy's flesh – and she wasn't home yet. The battle was still on and, with each hour that passed, the climax was drawing nearer.

25

HMS Furious, 20 April. Hob Gamble had snatched a cuppa on his way down to his cabin after the debriefing but, in spite of opening the punkah fully above his bunk he could not sleep. It was 1620 already and, though whacked by the constant ASW sorties, he could not arrest the turmoil in his tired brain as it relived the events of the past hours. Perhaps the fundamental truths of the funeral service were disturbing him – if so, he was not the only man to be affected, because afterwards Osgood had come up to see him.

Maybe the proximity of death was the reason why the ship's minute chapel had been packed for Holy Communion this morning; for the first time that he could remember, sailors and officers knelt unselfconsciously in large numbers before the altar rail. They had watched those stiff, flag-draped bundles on the quarterdeck slipping over the transom to splash into the foaming wake: their messmates, most of them in bits, many nameless, unidentifiable. But the burial service had provoked not only grief but hatred; those dead messmates were bundling over the side because of a brutal tyranny which had to be resisted and overthrown.

When the last body had vanished, the captain had asked them to remain on the quarterdeck. He told them, simply, of what lay ahead: their passage to Guz was certain to be hazardous – and no one must let up. He thanked all of them – from the junior seaman and the MEM, the Sea Harrier and chopper pilots, to the ops room crew; from the junior cooks, sick bay tiffy and stewards to the wardroom officers – for fighting the ship through. He reminded them not to expect too much when they got home: Plymouth was less damaged than at first feared, but lawless minorities were causing civil strife. And, he repeated, they weren't home yet.

After the bugler had sounded the Last Post they left the quarterdeck in silence. As the clear notes floated across the ocean, the men felt the tension of the past terrible days and nights suddenly released. They had dispersed for'd silently, no man speaking.

On the way to the wardroom, Hob had been approached by Osgood. His open face looked strained and anguished.

'You know Petty Officer Kotta's been killed, sir?'

'Yes.' Hob tried to sound optimistic: 'Don't let that influence your defence.' He had promised to be Osgood's 'prisoner's friend'.

'Sir?'

'Yes, Ozzie.' They stood in the corner of the flat and the aircrewman was talking softly.

'If I –' He hesitated, fumbling for words: 'If I don't get back, sir ... and Gwen Fane's all right. Tell her ...'

Hob nodded but remained silent.

'Tell her nothing's changed for me, sir, will you? If we survive this lot, they'll take me to barracks. I won't be seeing her.'

'I'll tell her, Oz.'

They had parted then, Osgood embarrassed as he mingled with the hands hurrying their way for'd.

And if he, Hob Gamble, was killed during his last lap, who would tell Allie? Death was breathing down their necks. Flying the cabs needed a fine touch and one hundred per cent concentration – and Hob knew he had no more to give. He held his hands above the blanket, stretching and splaying his fingers, watched the trembling in them. If only he could sleep. It was already 1625.

With only five cabs left, they were flying in sorties of two aircraft, to allow the third crew a double shift of sleep. The ssk line M had proved to be very much in evidence early this morning. The screen and the helos had accounted for three and, though several submarines had fired torpedoes, the foxers had dealt with them, the fish exploding harmlessly in the wakes. The afternoon ssk line N, during his sortie two hours ago, had been much more determined, but with no hits because Druce turned away at the crucial moment. They had scored two more submarine kills, though undoubtedly some had got away.

In four hours, *Furious* should be nearing the Falls, the light-ship at the entrance to the west-bound lane through the Strait of

Dover. CINCCHAN was waiting there with his Belgian, Dutch and RN sweepers – or what was left of them. Mines and enemy aircraft capable of dodging UKADGE were the final hazards to survive before reaching home and Allie. Hob turned on his side, drowsiness at last overcoming him ... and from somewhere far off he heard the summons of the rattlers.

At the bugler's imperious call to action stations he heaved himself from his bunk, flung on his jacket, slipped on his overalls. He stepped into the flat as the first torpedo struck.

Furious was hit by two torpedoes. The third ran wild. The fourth passed ahead and exploded in *Phoebe's* foxer. Hob had almost reached the briefing room when he sensed that the carrier was slowing down. The lights dimmed, then came on again as she began to heel rapidly. They were waiting for orders when Little F came through on the internal loop:

'All aircraft, take off *at the rush*!'

826 was the second cab to be readied. Hob ignored the pre-flight checks, and ran her up without the marshal. Trevellion was standing on the wings of his bridge. His unlit pipe jammed in his mouth, Old Chough was saluting his pilots for the last time. If only the Harriers could have been scrambled too, but there was no room on that twisted after deck.

Under the influence of the worsening list, 826 started sliding towards the side. The marshal yelled at them – the cab had not been refuelled yet. But Hob gave her full torque, lifting her as her port wheel scraped the lip. The angry waters jerked beneath them and then he was clear of the carrier's aerials – up and away. The HCO was through to Dunker.

'Get to hell out of it! Make for *Zuiderkruis*.'

'What are the other cabs doing?' Hob rapped.

'They've been refuelled,' Dunker said. 'Making for the Kentish coast.'

Where was *Zuiderkruis*? Hob peered to his left but couldn't spot the Dutch fast combat ship. As he clawed for height to bring 826 to the north-east astern of Mother, he caught his breath.

The carrier was fifteen hundred feet below them, turning full circle. A monstrous gash showed on her port quarter where one

178

torpedo had struck. Further for'd below the side lift, the second torpedo had blown a hole the size of a London bus in her side. Flames and smoke were pouring from it and fire parties were crawling like ants about the flight deck, trailing their snaking hoses behind them.

Over to the west, the frigates were firing at the missiles, sea-skimmers streaking in low. Time and time again the missiles slewed clear at the last second, diverted by ECM. He saw the flash on *Penelope*'s bridge, the tell-tale orange smoke and the wads of black fumes and sparks spilling from her innards. Below the cab, he saw the missile strike against the island, abaft *Furious*' bridge.

He could watch no longer: Old Fury was like an ex-champ, stubborn, proud, refusing to go down. Her list seemed to be steadying at about twenty-five degrees. *Goeben* and *Athabaskan* were turning at speed, heeling outwards, firing with everything they had . . . and then, as the fuel tank indicator began flashing, Grog shouted, cracking Hob's eardrums.

'There she is! *Zuiderkruis!*'

Four miles away, perhaps: up sun. Hob kept her in manual and chopped her back. The Dutchman was ready for him, had steadied up and was butting into the force five that had got up.

'Ready in the back, harnesses?'

'Yeah – strapping in,' Dunker called. 'Well done, Hob.'

Minutes later her wheels touched. He cut the engines, slammed on the rotor brake, as the Dutch handlers began slithering beneath the slowly revolving blades . . .

Hob never knew what happened next. There was a shrieking, whistling sound, a blinding flash, the crack and heat of an explosion. The cab, still with its rotors revolving, crashed, the undercarriage crumpling, as the flames on the flight deck of the Dutchman began engulfing her. She slid, toppling sideways briefly before tumbling over the side. Her blades caught in the netting.

'*Brace, brace, brace!*' Hob yelled.

The world spun round the trapped helicopter crew; they heard the swish of beating propellors. Torrents of water were deluging upon Hob as he groped for his window. The cab was upside down.

Hob tugged at his harness, but could not free it. Grog was getting out. Dunker Davies was going too, but Hob could not free himself, his harness jammed in the patent lock. Now tearing frenziedly at his harness, he was fighting for breath as the sea began to claim him. He was choking, he could fight no more . . . he saw Allie distinctly for a moment . . . then he felt powerful hands beneath his armpits, glimpsed the gleam of a blade flashing at his harness.

He heard Osgood shout, felt himself being hauled upwards, being shoved through the window. The aircrewman was scrambling, half-swimming, kicking and threshing towards his own side door. The cruel, dark sea was all round Hob, smothering, roaring, drowning him. He could hold his breath no longer; then suddenly everything stopped. He heard the sound of breaking waves. An arm was about him; Grog was yanking at the inflating tag. Hob, feeling his consciousness going, made a desperate effort to retain his senses.

Grog slid him into the survival raft which they all carried on their backs. The second pilot lashed the two of them together and it slowly dawned on Hob that the sun was out. They were on their own – and alive.

Of the helicopter, there was no trace: nor of Dunker, nor of Osgood.

26

North Sea, 20/21 April. The quietness, the utter loneliness was what they found the most unnerving. Grog had secured both the survival rafts together and, in his semi-consciousness, Hob heard him shouting above the breaking waves. His voice bore a forced cheerfulness which began to irritate Hob's throbbing headache. That Dunker and Osgood had both disappeared was a shocking thing which Hob's mind could still not accept.

'For God's sake!' Hob yelled. And in the silence which followed he heard only the rhythmic chuckling of the breaking waves. He lay back more securely into his survival raft, checked that his homing beacon was still functioning.

'You've not got your bleeper switched on?' he shouted. 'Not wasting its batteries.'

'Yeah, Hob. Okay, mine's off.'

Together, by their common cord, they floated with the swell, lurching to the crests for a glimpse of the endless horizon; swirling down to wallow in the troughs. And then, on an upward swoop, Hob saw the trail of low-down smoke, yellow and brown against the rose-tinted clouds of dusk.

'That's Old Fury,' Grog said. 'Bloody miracle – she's still afloat.'

'Old Chough'll get her home,' Hob said. 'He won't let the bastards have her.'

'I thought I saw *Zuiderkruis*,' Grog said, 'to the northward.'

They paddled their tiny survival rafts round to face the northern horizon. When they reached the crests, they saw her, smoke pouring from her.

'She's sinking,' Grog said.

During the next half-hour they caught sight of the fast combat ship intermittently, until finally they saw her founder: her stubby bows reared skywards, her stem poking above the jagged horizon-line, like a shark's fin ... she was gone.

'Well, Hob – we'd better settle for the night. They're bound to hear us soon. Mini-flares ready?'

But it was hard to keep up their spirits. As the crimson sun sank below the wavetops, the cold crept into them, numbing the very marrow of their bones. A Nimrod passed low on the horizon, flying eastwards, and Grog discharged a mini-flare. They followed the trajectory of the pathetic little red star; watched it falling, to vanish into the waves which were now getting up with the increasing wind.

'She's too far off.'

While twilight merged into night they started singing, repeating their repertoire of bawdy wardroom ditties and hymns and nursery rhymes. And when it was dark, the sparkling froth glistening down the wave-backs provided the light-giving phosphorescence which kept hope alive. Hob tried to recall the survival drill which had been knocked into him so often. The loss of heat would bring on the first symptoms of exposure – they *must* be alert for the creeping miasma of exposure – a sluggishness in the mind, drowsiness, an inclination to surrender – and they began singing again, desperately, their voices drowned by the mounting seas.

They decided to take it in turns to attempt sleep. The interminable night refused to pass: they broke up the endless hours by trying not to consult their wrist-watches; by nibbling at their emergency rations only after each four-hour spell had lapsed; and then Hob, half-asleep, heard Grog calling him:

'Look, Hob, first light.'

They cheered feebly and lay back, spinning their rafts round towards the east: they watched the silver streak, barely perceptible at first, steal like a thief into the dawn. To the westward the night clouds rolled slowly back while twilight broke, until at 0320 they were convinced that night was turning into another day. They celebrated with a square of chocolate and by singing Old Fury's marching-song 'Devon, Devon by the sea' which the volunteer band thumped out at colours on the flight deck during those far-off days of peace.

At 0730 they felt a glimmer of warmth when the sun shone balefully through the cirrus. Their spirits rose but the North Sea remained a cold, unfriendly place. At 0830 they had a biscuit each for breakfast; while they brooded, hunger still gnawing at them, Grog suddenly sat upright in his raft.

'Bloody hell, I'm seeing things.'

But on the next crest they both spotted the cross-trees of a small boat floundering in the seas.

'Flare!' yelled Grog.

Hob tore at his red pack, fumbled with the mini-flare, nipped it into the firing tube, snapped at the trigger. Grog was frenziedly following suit and together they watched the two red stars shooting to their summits, then curling downwards, falling, falling. They heard the chug-chug of diesels and yelled in unison until their lungs would burst; the craft came abeam, began drawing away; Hob blew frenziedly on his whistle. Grog loosed off another flare.

The craft sheered suddenly. They watched her turn towards them, saw her blunt bows – then up came her square, white bridge, pocked red where the rust slashed.

They heard the sharp, East Anglian accents as the heaving lines plopped about their heads. They looked up to see the sailors' weather-beaten, bearded faces, grinning down at them:

'Hold on, mates, we've got 'un.'

Breydon Water was one of those ugly, functional supply boats which the off-shore oil industry had engendered. She was on passage to the platforms when, an hour ago, her skipper had picked up the warning of enemy air attacks. He had learned to ignore the air raid alerts, but had not counted upon running across a swamped landing craft of RN survivors, and now he had picked up a couple of fliers from the same aircraft carrier.

In the saloon beneath the bridge, Hob and Grog were stripped off and given blankets. The warmth and hot tea revived them, but the other survivors from *Furious*, oil-streaked and shocked, remained uncommunicative. The bosun came in and poured them all stiff tots of rum, while a deckie brought them sizzling chunks of bacon and slices of fried bread. The Royal Marine sergeant moved up on the bench to make room for the two newcomers:

'Lieutenant Gamble, aren't you, sir? Our SPLOT?'

'Was,' Hob smiled ruefully. 'What's happened to our ship?'

deterrent had so far saved humanity from the worst; whether it would continue to do so, the world would soon know.

Layde peered upwards at the indigo bowl where Venus flickered, brilliant, in the west.

He sighed bitterly: survival now depended upon the sub-mariners.